THE STONE GIVER

Buffy Andrews

Published by Prism Book Group
ISBN-13: 978-1537549613
ISBN-10: 1537549618
First Edition, 2016
Published in the United States of America
Contact info: contact@prismbookgroup.com
http://www.prismbookgroup.com

DEDICATION

To my friend Sharon, founder of www.causearipple.com.
Thank you for providing the inspiration for this story. I love you
bunches and bunches!

To all those who served in the military. Thank you for your
service.

ACKNOWLEDGEMENTS

I thank God for His love, understanding, and guidance and for the incredible gifts He has given me.

I thank my husband, Tom, and my sons Zach and Micah for their love and support. I love you more than you'll ever know.

I thank my editor, Jacqueline Hopper, and my publisher, Joan Alley, who helped bring *The Stone Giver* to the world.

I thank Beth Vrabel for her excellent editing and always great advice. I couldn't do it without you!

I thank my sisters Dawn Beakler, Cindy Andrews, and Tania Nade for their abundant love.

I thank Robin Bohanan, Kris Ort, Laura Schreiber, Stacey Zambito, Shonna Cardello, Lilli Horn, Renee Maderitz, Bonnie Lerman and many others for their endless encouragement, hugs, and smiles.

And I thank you, my readers, for allowing me to share God's gift with you. I wish you a life of love and laughter.

Blessings always,

Buffy

CHAPTER ONE

Jack looked down at his legs. They were gone. A river of blood formed under him. He writhed in agony as the searing pain coursed through his broken body. Bloodcurdling screams boiled around him.

Nate?

Where was his best friend? He struggled to lift his head and looked to the right. He spotted Nate a few feet away, his body mangled and twisted into a bloody heap. Nate was dead.

Jack's body shook and sweat soaked his hospital sheets as the reoccurring nightmare choked him. He felt slender arms around him. *Her* arms cradling him, and he grabbed her soft shoulders and sobbed into her chest. She was his life raft, and he clung to her, gasping for air as he relived the desert hell. The blinding flashes. The screams. The smell of death.

"Breathe, Jack," Zara said. "Breathe. You're safe. With me. It's okay. You're okay. Just breathe."

Zara rocked him in her arms as if he were a baby that needed comfort and love. "That's it. Just breathe. Nice and easy. Everything's going to be okay. You're here with me."

Tears pooled in Zara's green eyes, and she once again caught herself before crossing the line she knew would be the end of her career. She almost—almost—kissed Jack on the head as she whispered soothing thoughts, trying to rescue him from the darkness in which he drowned.

Jack's breathing slowed, and his sobs lessened. Zara eased him back down on the mattress. The heartless beast that stole Jack's nights was gone for now, but they both knew he'd be back. And Zara knew she had to leave. She needed to save herself as much as she needed to save Jack, and she couldn't do both.

She reached into her pocket and pulled out the heart-shaped stone she'd spotted while sitting on the park bench the night before, when she'd been deep in thought. She'd looked down at her feet, and there it was, the most perfect heart-shaped rock she'd ever seen. Tan with specks of black.

Her chin wobbled, and she mashed her lips together. The rock reminded her of Johnny. Her brother had collected rocks. Once, they were at the river picking up rocks and throwing them into the water to see whose went farther.

"Look what I've found," Johnny had yelled. "A heart-shaped rock!" He'd stuffed the smooth, black rock into his shorts pocket, and Zara never saw it again.

"What do I want with a stupid stone?" Jack whipped the heart-shaped stone Zara had given him against the wall. "I lost my legs fighting this war, and you think a stupid stone is going to make me feel better?"

Anger boiled inside of Jack like lava. He hated everyone, but he hated himself more. Zara had been caring for him since he arrived at the medical center, and despite her vow not to get too close to her patients, she had slipped with Jack. At twenty-eight, he was only a couple years older.

She wanted to comfort him, to take away his pain. But his war wounds festered and had spread beyond his physical losses. He'd lost more than his legs the day his tank hit a roadside bomb in southern Afghanistan. He'd lost himself.

Zara's chin trembled, and she turned to see the stone hit the wall and fall to the floor. She walked over and picked it up. It was broken in two, a jagged break down the middle. She turned and went back to Jack. She stared into his steely brown eyes and laid the broken heart on his tray table next to a pitcher of water.

Jack's nostrils flared, and he clenched his teeth. His face turned as red as the apple on the tray in front of him. "Stones are made of minerals. When they're crushed, they turn to sand. I hate sand."

Jack raked his fingers through his curly, dark hair. "Listen, Nurse *Buttinsky*. If it's not a magic stone and can't bring back my legs, what good is it?"

Zara tried to ignore the "Nurse Buttinsky" comment, but it pierced her heart. "It's a reminder."

"Of what? Losing my legs? Of being a cripple the rest of my life?" He whipped back the sheet to show his stumps. "Does it look like I need a reminder?"

Zara bit her bottom lip. "I just want you to have it, that's all."

Jack watched Zara leave, her blonde corkscrew curls bouncing as she walked. He liked her a lot. Too much. From the moment she'd walked into his hospital room to care for him, his heart fluttered. He hadn't felt that flutter since he was fifteen, and it scared him to be feeling it now. He'd never have a chance with someone of her caliber, he thought. What would she want with a man with no legs?

Still, he wondered about her. A quick glance at her naked ring finger told him she wasn't married. Then again, no ring didn't always mean no man. Maybe she was married and didn't wear the ring at work. Or maybe she wasn't married but had a steady. Surely, a woman who looked like she'd stepped off the cover of Cosmo had to have a boyfriend, he figured. She probably had guys fighting to take her out. Why would she care about him? A cripple. A guy with no legs.

He punched the bed again. He hammered it so hard and so often that the mattress was dented. He pretended it was the enemy's face. Punching it made him feel good, his rage popping like a pierced balloon, the air escaping at once.

He tried to close his eyes, but he hated the darkness. Every time he closed his eyes, he'd see the explosion. The blinding flashes. Flying and flipping through the air. Landing and realizing his legs were gone. Blood soaking the ground under him. His team yelling his name. The excruciating pain. Nate a heap of bloody flesh.

He didn't remember the flight to Kandahar, Afghanistan, then to Landstuhl Regional Medical Facility in Germany, and finally to the U.S. His last memories were of being put on a helicopter, an oxygen mask being placed over his mouth, and a needle going into his arm. Eight days later, he woke up in Walter Reed Medical Center with stumps. He learned he'd flat-lined twice.

He wondered why the medics didn't just let him die.

Zara pulled out of the hospital parking garage for the last time. She didn't dare look back, too afraid she'd change her mind and stay. But she knew she'd made the right choice. She had a lot of things she had to work through. One of them was Jack.

Zara had feelings for him a nurse ought not to have for a patient, and she was pretty sure he had feelings for her too. She saw it in his lingering glances and the way his eyes pierced hers. It was almost as if he could see right through them.

She wasn't sure what had drawn her to Jack. He was needy, and insecure, and afraid. She tried to fight her feelings, but it was like trying to hold back a weak dam from breaking. Eventually, it would crumble and carry both of them away. She had to stop it before it did.

Maybe I shouldn't have given Jack the stone, she thought. It was silly of her to think it would mean anything to him. He wasn't Johnny. But she wanted him to have it before she left. She knew Jack thought his limitations were outside of him, and she hoped in time he'd see they were really on the inside. He needed to focus on what he had left, not what he'd lost. But Zara knew that would take time and he'd have to learn it on his own.

She was intimate with the stages of grief, and it wasn't always a neat, orderly process. Sometimes people didn't move through the stages in order—denial, anger, bargaining, depression, and acceptance. Sometimes they skipped stages. She had one patient who even bounced back and forth between the stages. Most, sooner or later, accepted the loss and worked through the emotional and physical pain and adjusted to life without their limbs and began to move on.

Jack's anger was the worst she'd seen. She wanted to tell him she understood his anger. She wanted to tell him that it could've been worse. He could've died like her brother. He too was killed by an IED. Johnny, a Marine sergeant, had been a bomb-disposal expert. He was on foot patrol in southern Afghanistan when he'd stepped on an IED that detonated with ten pounds of homemade explosive. The blast threw him into the air, and he'd landed on his back in a ditch.

Because dismounted troops walked with their weapons held out in front of them, when they stepped on an IED, they often lost both legs as well as the extended arm. In Johnny's case, the explosion blew off his legs and severed his right hand.

Zara cursed the orders for U.S. troops to get out of their protective armored vehicles and patrol on foot whenever possible. While the order might have been hailed as an essential counterinsurgency tactic used to get closer to the people and pick up intelligence, the number of severe injuries had jumped exponentially. The Taliban insurgents were making bombs using plastic buckets packed with explosive ammonium nitrite fertilizer, and the crude components made the bombs more difficult to detect than those made with metal parts.

She knew Jack's story, knew he blamed himself for the explosion that killed the gunner, his best friend. Jack had been driving an armored vehicle on a routine mission back to base. The vehicle had been fitted with a mine roller, but the Taliban outsmarted it. The insurgents set up the IED to explode under the vehicle by burying the pressure plate several yards ahead of the bomb. By the time the mine roller hit the plate, it was too late. The explosion, strong enough to knock down concrete walls and bend metal, tossed the vehicle like a toddler done playing with a toy.

Zara's cell phone rang. She pulled over to the curb. "Hi, Mom. What's up?"

"Zara, what are you thinking?"

Zara cleared her throat. "Mom, look, I'm fine. I just needed a change. It's not like I'm walking away. I've completed my service obligation. I just need time to figure out what I want to do next."

"But you didn't have to resign," her mom said. "You're a darn good Army nurse. Why are you throwing that away?"

"I'm not throwing anything away," Zara snapped. She was tired of having this conversation with her mom. "I'll always be a military nurse, but I might want to do something else."

"Like what?"

"I don't know. That's what I need to figure out. Look, Mom, I gotta go. I pulled over to the curb to talk to you, and I really need to get home. I'll call you later."

Zara knew her mom didn't understand her decision. She hadn't mentioned her growing feelings for Jack. That was her secret, and she kept it safe, locked in her heart away from ridicule, and lectures, and pointing fingers.

CHAPTER TWO

Jack glanced at the broken stone on the tray. He reached for it, but it was too far away. He felt terrible he'd treated Zara so badly. After all, she cared for him night after night. Zara was the one who calmed him when he woke up from a dream in which he was playing basketball with his buddies in the park. In his dream, he was whole. When he woke up and reality came rushing back, he started to hyperventilate.

Zara often gathered him in her arms and held his head tight against her chest. Sweat soaked his sheets, and he gulped mouthfuls of air. "It's okay," she'd whisper. "You're safe. Breathe with me." And she rocked him in her arms until his body stopped shaking and his breathing slowed.

He reached down to feel his stubs, which were covered in compression bandages. They reminded Jack of giant socks. He knew the dressings helped keep the swelling down and increased the blood pressure at the site of the amputation. At least, that's what Zara had explained to him. He liked how she explained everything she was doing, as if it helped her as much as it helped him.

"I'm giving you an antibiotic. We need to take care of that infection caused by all the dirt that was driven deep into your wounds and soft tissue." And, "Stretching your limb stump is important. It helps with the circulation."

She was there when the phantom limb pain caused by the amputated nerve endings misfiring made him writhe in agony. It felt like someone was holding a blowtorch to his stumps. He cursed the burning sensation and shooting pain, telling himself he'd have been better off dead. It was Zara who worked tirelessly to control his pain so he could sleep.

Whenever he'd come back from physical therapy feeling defeated, she'd remind him how important it was to strengthen his bones and muscles elsewhere in his body to compensate for the missing limbs. She was always so positive.

Jack wondered where Zara was. She should have been here by now. He wanted to apologize for his behavior the night before. He shouldn't have thrown the stone.

Jack heard a knock on his door. He thought that was strange— people usually just came in. "It's open."

A guy that looked to be about Jack's age wearing jeans, a screened tee, and a Red Sox baseball cap came in. He walked over to Jack's bed. "Hi." He held out his hand to shake Jack's. "My name's Tom. I thought I'd stop by."

Jack's thick brows furrowed. "Do I know you?"

Tom shook his head. "And I don't know you, but I do know what you're going through."

Jack's eyes widened. He could feel his anger building, and he wanted to stop it before it spun out of control. "Don't tell me that. Don't tell me you know what it feels like to be me."

Tom rubbed his neck. "I didn't say I knew what it felt like to be you. I said I know what you're going through. Three years ago, I was the one laying in that bed."

Jack ran his fingers through his hair and sucked in his breath. "I would've never known. You walk like you have real legs."

Tom nodded to a nearby chair. "Mind if I sit?"

"Sure. Whatever. Sorry, man."

Tom pulled the chair over to the side of the bed.

Jack sniffed. "So how'd you lose yours?"

"IED. Just like you. There was an IED we hadn't detected. We swept it three times, even rolled it with a mine roller. I stepped on it, and it took off both my legs right on the spot."

"How'd you get through it?"

"It took me awhile," Tom said. "I was angry for a long time. And then one day, it hit me like a bomb." He held up his hand. "No pun intended. I had to make a decision. I could either sit back and give up and let everyone take care of me, or get busy with what I had. I decided to get busy."

Tom paused. "You know, some guys come back and their brains are all messed up. They don't remember their spouses or families. I can live without my legs. But those guys with brain injuries—they've got it worse. That motivated me to move on. I was happy that wasn't me. Just wait until you get your prostheses."

"What's it like walking on those?" Jack asked, reaching down to touch his stumps.

Tom pulled up his jeans, revealing a high-tech device attached to a white leather sneaker. "My wife tells me I have the sexiest legs of any guy she's ever met."

Jack laughed. "So you're married?"

Tom nodded. "Yeah. Her name's Jen. We were engaged when it happened, though."

"And she stuck with you?"

"Yep! She flew in from California right away and never left. Gave up her job to help me. Now we're an old married couple. She teaches school, and I'm in school. Always wanted to help kids, so I'm studying to become a guidance counselor."

"Cool! So the legs. What's it like?"

Tom pulled his jeans down over his prosthetic leg and sat up. "It was weird at first. The best part, though, was being back at eye level with everyone around me. And I never thought I'd run again. But I have special legs for that, which is pretty neat."

"They can do that? Give you different legs for different things?"

"Absolutely! One guy I met played ice hockey, and he got artificial legs with skates attached."

Jack shook his head. "I had no idea."

Tom's gaze moved to the broken stone sitting on the tray. "Can I ask you something?"

Jack nodded.

Tom pointed to the stone. "What's that?"

"Will you hand it to me?" Jack asked.

Tom dropped the two pieces into Jack's open hand. Jack held them together to make it whole.

"It was a heart-shaped stone. A nurse—her name's Zara—gave it to me."

Tom listened as Jack told him what had happened after Zara gave him the stone. How he'd thrown it against the wall in a rage. How he knew he'd hurt her feelings, but what the heck did he want with a stupid stone made out of sand? Jack unleashed his thoughts, and they roiled and rolled into one big thunderous wave that eventually crashed into a sobbing mess. He buried his face in his hands. "I failed my brothers," he muttered between sobs. "I let them down."

Tom stood and touched Jack's shoulder. He stared into Jack's face. "You didn't fail, Jack. Wounds are not failures. You didn't get wounded because you were a coward or weak."

Jack sniffed, and Tom handed him a tissue. "Remember, anger is energy. Use that energy to build a new life. Yes, it might not be the one you'd imagined, but take it from me it can still be a pretty good one."

They talked some more, and before Tom left, he said he'd send Jack some glue in case he wanted to mend his broken heart.

Jack clutched the stone pieces in the palm of his hand when a nurse walked into the room. She wasn't Zara.

It was Zara's first full day unemployed, and she planned to spend it packing. She promised her best friend, Laura, she'd meet her at the bar later.

Zara stood in her living room and scanned her apartment. She couldn't believe how much stuff she had accumulated in the last five years. It seemed like she had a lifetime of junk. She grabbed one of the empty boxes she'd stashed in the corner and picked up the leather photo album sitting on the coffee table. She'd bought the album after she moved to Maryland. While most of her friends took photos with their phones, Zara was old school. She preferred pointing her Nikon and holding the physical photos in her hands. They were more permanent, harder to erase by accident.

She opened the album and smiled at the young girl staring back at her. I look so young, she thought. Her curly mop was straighter then. She'd stopped battling it with hair relaxers several months ago, after Johnny died. As a sort of an ode to him. Johnny had curly hair too. It was the one physical trait they shared. They'd inherited the curls from their dad, who managed his with a close crop haircut.

Whenever Zara thought about Johnny being blown apart, she felt as if there was a boulder sitting on her chest, crushing her heart into a million pieces. Her heart physically hurt.

Zara turned the pages, traveling back in time. She smiled at the photo of her ex-boyfriend, Chris, and her dressed as a hunter and Bambi for Halloween. He wore camouflage pants and shirt and an orange hunting cap and vest. She wore a sexy brown dress covered with white spots made out of paper. She and Chris couldn't decide between these outfits and a firefighter and Dalmatian, so they wrote the two ideas down and dropped them into a cup, and Chris picked one.

Zara liked Chris a lot, but they both realized over time they were more friends than lovers, and they both deserved better. He was a physical therapist, and they became fast friends after meeting at the local bar. He was a perfect mix of tough guy and teddy bear. One thing led to another, and they soon found themselves a couple.

Eventually, Chris broke it off. He'd met someone, and he wanted to explore where the relationship could go. Zara couldn't blame him. She knew it was only a matter of time before one of them walked away. And she was sort of glad it was Chris. She hated being the one to break things off. That was two years ago, and Zara hadn't been with anyone since. She dated some, but none of them made her insides turn to liquid. Until Jack.

She felt guilty thinking about Jack that way. Her growing feelings for him prompted her to leave sooner rather than later. At first, she told herself she was confusing pity for romantic interest, but she could only lie to herself for so long. She had fallen for Jack, and there wasn't a darn thing she could do about it. Still, she didn't want Jack to feel as if she'd abandoned him.

Maybe he wouldn't care that she'd left, but Zara had a feeling he would. So she wrote a letter and asked the nurse who replaced her to deliver it. She knew Jack would be expecting her today, and she wanted to make sure he didn't give up on himself.

In some ways, Zara felt she had let Johnny down. He was a few years younger, and she'd always looked out for him, protected him as best she could. When they were kids and the school bully made fun of Johnny's lisp, Zara was the one who gave the bully a bloody lip. When Johnny's first love broke his heart, Zara was the one who helped him mend. But she couldn't protect him when he'd stepped on the pressure plate of a roadside bomb.

Zara closed the photo album and packed it in the box. She'd buy a new album after she moved. She'd rented a storage unit to stash this box and the rest of her belongings. The place she had leased in Florida for the next six months was furnished. She figured she'd give herself half a year to decide what her next move would be.

She walked over to the bookcase beside her TV and pulled out the books, making two piles—those she'd keep and those she'd give away. The keep pile was double the size of the give-away pile. She hated parting with books, especially those given to her as gifts. She loved getting lost in a good book, and lately her genre of choice was romance. She needed the happily-ever-after endings like she needed air. They kept her going when darkness took her by the throat and choked the slivers of happiness she'd managed to gather.

She pulled out the last book Johnny had given her—*Pride and Prejudice*. She opened the cover to read the note he wrote.

Zara, Just like Lizzie Bennett, you're strong and smart and you know what you want. So go for it. Love, Johnny.

Tears pooled in Zara's eyes. She sniffed as she traced Johnny's name with her fingertip. She missed him. Every Christmas, he'd buy her a book with a strong female protagonist. He knew how much she loved books, and he'd give her ones featuring protagonists that reminded him of her. There was Jo March from *Little Women* and Jane Eyre. These books were her favorites, and she'd never part with them—ever.

Zara grabbed another empty box from the corner. She'd decided to take the books Johnny gave her along to Florida. She wanted them close by.

Zara finished packing the books and checked the time on her cell phone. She told Laura she'd meet her at seven. Another hour and she'd have to get ready. She figured an hour would be enough time to finish the living room. That left the kitchen cabinets and her closet. She'd packed up her dresser the night before.

She glanced at the stack of boxes in the corner. She'd been collecting them at the grocery store for weeks. Maybe she'd stop by on her way to the bar and see if it had any more, she thought. She liked egg boxes best because they were so sturdy. A few more of those would be good for the glassware.

One good thing about the move was that it forced Zara to evaluate the physical contents of her life. There were so many things she thought she needed and bought, only to realize they were wants, not needs. Like the expensive basket sitting next to the sofa she used to hold magazines, a reminder of money that could've been better spent.

Life happens. Priorities change. She changed. She knew she wasn't the same girl who'd stepped inside the military hospital five years ago. It seemed as if it was a lifetime ago. She'd seen so much pain and suffering—and joy.

Yes, joy.

Whenever darkness had its grimy hands around her throat, she'd remember those who'd made it. Patients who went from spending months in a hospital bed without being able to do anything on their own to sprinting down the hallways at the medical center with their curved carbon-fiber prosthetic legs. They were the reason she went to work every day.

She opened the wooden box she kept on her nightstand and took out the smiley face pill puzzle she'd stashed inside. During Johnny's last visit, he talked her into getting a kid's meal with him. "Oh, come on, Z." He'd laughed. "For old time's sake. Remember how Mom used to take us for kids' meals after swim lessons every week?"

She blinked back tears as the sweet memory of them playing with the plastic puzzles rushed back to her. Zara tilting the toy, trying to get the four tiny silver balls into the holes. She'd get one in. Maybe two. But just as she'd manage to ease a third one in, one of the other balls would pop out. Johnny, on the other hand, could always do it. Four balls in four holes all at the same time. Perfect.

Zara turned the puzzle over in her hand. She felt as if her life was like the pill puzzle. She had several loose balls in her life, and she was trying desperately to get them into the holes where they belonged all at the same time. But just as she struggled with the puzzle, she struggled with this. Would she ever been able to do it? She wondered. Would the holes in her life ever be filled? She didn't know, but she knew she had to keep trying. She owed Johnny that.

"You keep practicing," Johnny had told her. "The next time I come home, I want to see all of the balls in the holes."

Zara tilted the puzzle, trying yet again. She didn't want to let Johnny down.

CHAPTER THREE

"Good afternoon, Jack." A middle-aged nurse with a round middle and thick arms smiled and walked over to his bed. "Zara left this for you." She held up an envelope. "And Tom said you needed some super-strength glue. I found some in the desk drawer." She held up the glue.

Jack shifted in his bed, placing the broken stone on his sheet. He took the envelope and the glue. "Where is Nurse Buttinsky, anyway?"

The nurse narrowed her dark eyes and pursed her thin, chapped lips. "What did you call her?"

Jack cleared his throat. "Zara. I mean Zara."

The nurse smiled. "That's better. And Zara's gone, so you're stuck with me."

Jack stiffened. "What do you mean she's gone?"

The nurse checked Jack's stumps. "I mean she left. For good. Got an honorable discharge. Guess she decided to do something different."

Jack shook his head. "But she didn't say anything."

The nurse pointed to the envelope. "Maybe that's her good-bye. Seeing you're the only patient she left a note for, there must've been something she wanted to tell you."

Jack looked at the black licorice lanyard and white identification badge dangling from the nurse's neck. He squinted to read her name. "Hi, Donna. I'm Jack Quinlan."

She winked. "I know who you are, sweetie."

"Oh, yeah. Sorry."

Donna checked his vital signs. "Looking good, Jack. How'd your visit with Tom go?"

Jack's mouth turned up at the ends. "I like him a lot. Couldn't believe when he pulled up his jeans and showed me his legs."

Donna smiled. "He's a good guy. He'll make a great guidance counselor. And a great dad."

Jack's eyes widened. "He didn't tell me he was going to have a kid."

"Yeah, he's due in about two months."

Jack chuckled. "You mean his wife's due."

"No, him. The baby's a boy."

The nurse and Jack laughed.

"Wow," Jack said, "a son. Bet he never thought that would be in the cards when he was lying in this bed."

Donna smoothed out Jack's sheet. "You're probably right. But there's one thing you should know about Tom and every other wounded vet who's walked out of here. They were determined. There's nothing more important than determination, Jack. I've seen it move mountains. Doesn't mean it wasn't tough. But those who made it never gave up."

Jack stared straight ahead, thinking about what Donna had just said.

Donna patted Jack's arm. "I'll be back in a bit. Give you some time alone to read your letter before going to physical therapy."

Man, Jack thought, Tom's doing so well. *Maybe it is possible to have a better future than I'd thought.*

He looked at the plain white envelope with *Jack Quinlan* written in blue ink on the front. He tried to peel back the flap, but it was glued shut. Instead, he ripped open the envelope, careful not to tear the letter. He took out the piece of paper and unfolded it.

Dear Jack,

Sorry I had to leave and won't be there to see you through the rehabilitation process. One of my greatest regrets is not being able to see you walk out the door on your prostheses. I know it seems impossible now, but trust me that if you work hard and listen to Pete, it will happen.

Please don't give up on yourself. There's a world out there that needs Jack Quinlan in it.

Remember, there's only one way for your dream to die and that's if you let it. Hold on to that dream and maybe one day we'll meet again.

Zara

Jack's lips quivered, and his chin wobbled. He tried to keep the tears at bay, but they busted loose like a sudden summer storm that pops up with little warning. He did have a dream. He wanted to walk again. And run. He wanted his independence. He wanted to be able to go anywhere and do anything. And he wanted to find Zara.

She had become more than his nurse—she'd become his friend. And, deep down, he'd wondered if they could be more. There was something about her that made him feel alive, and he hadn't felt alive in a long time. He wanted to hold on to that emotion, bottle it, and keep it forever. And he could've sworn she felt something too. He sensed it in her touch. Her smile. The sensation brushed him like a soft, sweet breeze on a summer day.

Donna walked in. "Are you all right, Jack?"

Jack sniffed. "I'm ready for therapy. And this time, I want to go down to the rehab gym on my own."

Zara found Laura at the bar and slid onto the stool next to her. "Sorry I'm late. I got caught up in packing."

Laura sipped her beer. "No biggie. I was just talking to Mike here." She pointed to the six-foot bartender with a goatee.

"What can I get you?" Mike asked.

"Gin and diet tonic."

"House gin okay?"

Zara nodded.

"So are you all packed?" Laura asked.

"Almost. I'll finish tomorrow."

"I can't believe you're leaving me." Laura pouted.

"I'll only be a phone call away, and you can visit anytime."

Zara thanked the bartender for the drink and took a sip. "Besides, you have Jude."

Laura danced in her seat. "True, I do. And he's amazing. Well, not as amazing as you, but…"

"Oh, stop it." Zara playfully tapped Laura's shoulder. "He is amazing, and you're perfect for one another. I hope I find what you two have some day."

Laura tossed some peanuts into her mouth. "Speaking of special people, what did Jack say when you told him you were leaving?"

"I didn't tell him. I wrote him a letter."

"Coward."

Zara shrugged. "It was easier that way. Besides, to him I'm Nurse Buttinsky. I only wrote him a note because I didn't want him to give up on himself."

"And because you like him," Laura added.

Zara sighed. "I hate myself for becoming emotionally attached to him. I've never allowed that to happen before."

"Maybe it's because he didn't have anyone," Laura said. "Most wounded soldiers have someone who stays with them during their time at the hospital. A parent, wife, or girlfriend. Someone. Jack had no one—except you."

Zara had thought about that. Wondered if that's why Jack had become a special case, as she'd described him to Laura. It's also why she felt guilty about leaving him.

She knew from the many hours she'd spent caring for Jack that he had no family. Raised by a single mom who died when he was eighteen, he was alone in the world. The military was the closest thing he had to family.

Once, Zara found him shaking and sweating so profusely he'd soaked his sheets. His fever of 104 made him confused. He'd thought Zara was his mother. "Why'd you pick him over me?" he'd asked. "I was your son."

Zara bit her bottom lip remembering the exchange, trying to explain to Jack she wasn't his mom but his nurse. After Zara managed to get Jack's fever under control, he apparently didn't remember the conversation. But Zara never forgot it.

Even as a young girl, Zara always wanted to feel needed, to have a purpose outside of herself. She needed to see something get better at her hand. And she worked tirelessly to make that happen. Week after week, month after month, year after year, she looked after the wounded coming back from war. Despite the best care she was able to provide, some didn't make it. She took their deaths personally. She wanted to save them all. Just like she wanted to save all of the feral cats that prowled her neighborhood growing up.

Zara remembered what her mom had told her. "Zara, honey. You can't save them all."

"I can try," Zara said. And she did.

Laura pushed her empty beer glass forward, signaling to the bartender she wanted another draft. She turned to Zara. "A penny for your thoughts."

"I was just thinking about all of the feral cats I tried to help growing up. I'd trap them, pay to have them neutered and vaccinated, then return them to the community. Mom thought I was crazy for spending all my birthday money and allowances trying to save homeless cats. But I knew if I helped one, it would in turn help them all. That over time, the feral cat population would diminish, and those returned to the community would be healthier."

Laura nodded. "Sounds sort of like the job you're leaving. Only instead of cats, you're helping to save soldiers. You help fix them up so they can return to the community and start over."

Zara laughed. "Well, never thought of it like that, but yeah. Sort of. And sometimes the cats that were friendly toward people were adopted. That was the best."

"Well," Laura said, "you always were a sucker for happily-ever-afters."

"True. I wonder if I'll ever find mine. I mean, I thought Chris might be it. I absolutely adored the guy. Still do."

"And he adores you," Laura said. "But there was no chemistry between you two. You were best friends. He's the type of guy you could take to a wedding and have a great time with, but not the guy you'd want standing beside you at the altar saying your vows."

"True. We could talk for hours, but when it came to intimacy, it fell flat. Weird how you can connect with someone with your heart and your mind, but if your bodies don't connect, you can't make them."

Laura sipped her beer. "And then there was Kevin. That was all spark. Sizzle hot! You guys were on fire together."

Zara laughed. "Yeah, Kevin was definitely an Oxytocin high. But there was no friendship beneath the intimacy, and that didn't work for me either. Geez, I sound like such a loser."

Laura playfully tapped Zara's shoulder. "You're not a loser. What you need is a guy you connect to with your mind and your heart, like Chris, and your body, like Kevin."

"Isn't three a crowd?" Zara joked.

"Not those three," Laura said. "You need all three to win. If you got the heart, and the mind, and the body, that's a trifecta. The winning combination."

Mike walked over. "See those guys sitting at the end of the bar? They bought you a shot. Do you want it, or should I tell them to get lost?"

Zara and Laura turned in the direction Mike pointed.

"You mean the two guys that look like they've just graduated from kindergarten?" Laura asked.

Mike smiled. "Yeah, them."

Zara sipped her drink. "Are they harmless?"

Mike nodded. "Pretty much. They started hanging out here a couple weeks ago—right after they turned twenty-one."

The girls laughed.

"Tell them we'll take a shot if they do one with us," Laura said. "That ought to give them something to brag to their friends about."

Mike walked down to relay the message, and the guys jumped off their bar stools and practically ran to Zara and Laura. Turned out Teddy—short for Theodore—and R.J.—short for Ryan James—were seniors studying at the local university.

Mike set up four shot glasses and filled them with Jack Daniel's. He handed a shot glass to each of them.

"One. Two. Three!" Laura shouted.

They each downed the shot and high-fived each other.

R.J. shook his head. "I think that was one drink too many." He started to sway and grabbed onto the back of Zara's chair.

"How are you guys getting home?" Zara asked.

"We walked here," Teddy said.

"Do you need help getting your friend home?" Laura asked.

"No. But I think I better get him out of here before he upchucks the hot wings he ate earlier."

Laura, Zara, and Mike watched as Teddy wrapped his arm around R.J. and helped him out the door.

"Something tells me that's one story they aren't going to brag about to their friends," Zara said.

CHAPTER FOUR

When Jack maneuvered his wheelchair through the doors and into the rehab gym, the therapists stopped what they were doing and applauded. It was the first time Jack had come down to the gym by himself, a monumental moment.

Pete, his therapist, intercepted him when he was halfway to his workout station. "You're doing great, Jack. Your upper body is getting stronger every day." He pointed to the stubs sticking out of Jack's black nylon shorts. "And your residual limbs are healing nicely. The swelling's going down."

"Good," Jack said. "After a dozen surgeries to clean out infections and dirt in my wounds, I'm ready to get my bionic legs."

Pete nodded. "Looks like that'll be any day now. And, Jack, don't be so hard on yourself. It usually takes one to two months after surgery until the limb is healed before patients are ready for their first fitting. What's it been? A little over a month?"

Jack looked at the large round clock on the wall and then back at Pete. "Forty nine days, three hours. Give or take a few minutes."

Pete shook his bald head. "Amazing."

Jack stared into Pete's steely blue eyes. "You never forget the moment your life changes forever."

Pete playfully tapped his shoulder. "But look how far you've come. Remember the first day I brought you down here? You sat on a mat in the center of the gym watching everyone around you."

"I remember. I felt like I was back in the barracks with all the teasing."

Pete laughed. "This place does have that feel to it. Ready to do some stump lifts?"

He helped Jack onto the mat table and provided resistance while Jack lifted his stumps, one at a time, in all four directions.

The Marine sharing Jack's mat table was a newbie. He was missing his legs too and one of his arms. "Do you ever feel like just giving up?"

Jack wiped the sweat off his face with a gym towel. "A time or two maybe. But someone once told me there's only one way for a dream to die, and that's if you let it."

His mat mate, who introduced himself as Kyle, nodded. "So what's your dream?"

Jack thought for a minute. "I want to stand at the altar and walk down the aisle with my wife."

Kyle nodded. "You got a girlfriend?"

Jack shook his head. "Maybe someday. What about you?"

"Used to but got a Dear John letter during basic training. Said she didn't want to be tied down. She's in college."

Jack pointed to Kyle's stumps. "What's your story?"

"Roadside bomb. I stepped on a pressure plate and ended up in a canal in rural Afghanistan."

"Listen to your PT," Jack advised. "He knows what he's doing."

"Jack!" Pete joked. "What did I hear you say? Your PT knows what he's doing?"

Jack smiled. "Don't let it go to your head, but yeah, you've brought me a long way." He turned to Kyle. "I could've killed Pete when he showed up at my bed ready to start therapy. It was a day or so after surgery, and I had wound VACs, a catheter bag, and a ton of lines going everywhere. And he showed up wanting to know what I could do."

Pete grinned. "No one gets better lying in bed and doing nothing."

"Yeah, yeah, yeah." Jack patted the mat. "You'll find it's easier to learn how to sit and roll on these mats than your hospital mattress. It's firmer."

Kyle watched as Jack did push-ups and Pete counted. When he was done, Pete shouted, "Give me ten more!"

When Jack finished his mat routine, he took a swig of water. Out of the blue he mumbled, "She left."

Pete looked around the gym, as if thinking Jack was referring to someone there. "Who?"

Jack took another swig. "Zara."

"Oh," Pete said. "Your nurse. I heard she was leaving. Where she'd go?"

Jack shrugged. "Don't know. I only learned she left when a different nurse walked into my room. Donna."

"Oh, I know her. Big woman." Pete held up his hands to emphasize big. "But a heck of a nice nurse."

Jack nodded. "Yeah, seems nice."

"But she's not Zara, is she?"

Jack shook his head. "No, she's not Zara."

"You liked her a lot, didn't you?"

Jack nodded. "I blew up at her yesterday. I planned to apologize when she came in today. I guess that'll never happen."

Jack shared the stone incident with Pete and told him what Zara had written in her letter.

Pete waved his hand. "It's never too late to say you're sorry, Jack. What would make Zara happy is you walking out of here."

"Some days, I feel like that's never going to happen." Jack mashed his lips together and pointed to a Marine walking with short prosthetic legs. "Josh got his stubbies already, and he arrived after me."

"Don't compare yourself to others," Pete advised. "Everyone's different. Josh's stumps healed a little quicker, that's all." Pete motioned to Jack's stumps. "They look good. I think your stitches will come out any day now. Just hang in there."

Jack scanned the rehab gym. "Well, it's not like I have a whole lot of places I can go."

When Jack returned to his room, he found his heart-shaped stone sitting on his tray. Someone had glued the two pieces together. He picked it up, careful not to break it again.

"So," Laura said. "Jude wants to move in together. Says we should buy a house. What do you think?"

Zara sipped her drink. "That's a tough one. But it doesn't matter what I think. What matters is how you feel about it. Does the idea of moving in with a guy, buying a house together with no real commitment, bother you? Have you even talked about marriage?"

"He feels the way I do," Laura said. "Having a piece of paper isn't essential anymore. I mean, marriage isn't as important as having a great relationship, and we have that. So what's the big deal?"

"So why not marry, then?" Zara asked.

"Ugh! You sound like my mom."

Zara grimaced. "I don't mean to go all "mom" on you. I just don't get this whole nearly wed trend. I guess I'm just old-fashioned. I want the guy to bend down on one knee and ask me to spend the rest of my life with him. And I want him to accept my quirky weirdness with love."

"Like I said, you always did love happily-ever-afters. Living together isn't as scary. It's less permanent. And you know I don't like depending on others."

"So you view any real commitment as a risky venture?" Zara asked.

"Yeah, I guess so. This seems like the perfect middle. Besides, if we live together, we'll get to see if we're really compatible."

"And he'll see that flip-flops and yoga pants make up more of your wardrobe than he'd originally thought." Zara laughed.

Laura flashed Zara her mean face. "It could keep us from making a big mistake."

"I just think it's too easy to walk away and not try to work things out," Zara said. "Having that piece of paper gives you the incentive to try harder when times get tough."

"Okay!" Laura threw up her arms. "I like having an escape hatch. There, I said it. But he does too."

Zara held up her finger. "One word. Prehab. Make sure you get something drawn up—who gets what if things don't work out. Remember what happened to Stephanie? A year turned into two, turned into five, and a dog and a kid later, they split. What a mess!"

"I'm hungry," Laura said. "For a greasy burger and fries."

"Way to change the subject!" Zara laughed. "Greasy burger and fries? I thought you were dieting. Your Instagram feed is all salads and sneakers."

Laura laughed. "Not tonight. I'm taking a break from my good-for-libido foods."

Zara laughed. "I hadn't realized that's how you were choosing foods."

"It was Jude's idea," Laura said. "He said foods that are good for your heart are also good for your libido. Did you know carrots are a well-known libido enhancer?"

Zara shook her head. "I eat a lot of those."

"We've been eating stuff like mustard greens, spinach, baby kale, and yams," Laura said.

"Do you think it's made a difference?" Zara asked.

"Honestly? No. But Jude swears it's done wonders for him, and it has kept my weight down. But I've been freakin' dying for a burger and fries since the other night when we went out to eat and got our usual salads. A woman at the table next to us was eating a big, beautiful, greasy burger, and I felt like a dog with my tongue hanging out waiting for her to drop a piece on the floor."

Zara laughed. "Well, I'm sure Mike has a greasy burger on the bar menu."

Zara loved hanging with Laura. She'd been her bestie since college, and when Zara moved to Maryland, Laura followed, taking a job teaching ninth-grade English in one of the inner-city schools. A fellow teacher introduced Laura to her brother, Jude. He was a financial analyst and a health nut. They'd hit it off immediately.

Zara was happy for her. Secretly, she'd hoped that Johnny and Laura would get together, but the timing never seemed right. Either he had a girlfriend or she had a boyfriend, and then he died and that was the end of that.

By the time Zara returned to her apartment, it was nearly midnight. She looked around, trying to figure out how much time it would take her to finish packing in the morning. She walked out onto her apartment balcony and looked up. A bright saucer moon and a sea of stars graced the sky.

So close and yet so far away.

CHAPTER FIVE

Donna bounced into Jack's room. "Today's the day!"

Jack looked up from his iPad. It was a gift from Tom. He'd been watching videos of amputees doing amazing things—running marathons, swimming, skydiving.

Donna opened the mini blinds, allowing sunshine to flood Jack's room. "Doc says the stitches can come out."

Jack punched the air. "Yeah! All right!" He turned his iPad around so Donna could see the screen. "I want to be like this guy." He tapped on the screen. "Guy was a triple amputee, and he ran a marathon. I want to do that."

"Then you will!" Donna patted him on the shoulder.

Jack turned off his tablet. "What makes you so sure?"

Donna stopped writing on her clipboard and looked at Jack. "Because you want it so badly. You know, Jack, I've been working with wounded soldiers for thirty years now, and the ones who make it are the ones who want to. Some never get better. And it's not because of their injuries or because their physical therapist was lousy—it's because they always played the victim. And victims never get better. So you have a choice to make. Play the victim and sit around, and complain, and sulk, or do something to get better."

Jack stared into space. "I think that's what Zara was trying to tell me. She said a dream only dies if you let it."

Donna nodded. "She's right. You have to make a decision about what you want your life to be. Yes, your legs are gone, but that doesn't mean your life is. You can either quit living and trying or work hard to overcome your disability and live the kind of life you want to live. You want to be like those amputees in those videos." She pointed to his iPad. "You can. But it's going to take hard work, and determination, and commitment. I can want it for you. Zara can want it for you. We don't matter. The only person who matters is you. How badly do you want it?"

Jack clenched his teeth. "Pretty darn bad."

"Then let's remove those stitches so the prosthetist can fit you for your legs."

Jack lay down, and Donna spread a folded blanket under his stumps. She sprayed his left limb with disinfectant and rubbed it with a gauze pad. "This shouldn't hurt. I don't expect blood, but if there is, I'll dab it with this." She held up a pad.

Holding tweezers in her right hand, Donna lifted the first knot slightly above Jack's skin. With the scissors in her other hand, she snipped the suture next to the knot, pulling the stitch through Jack's skin and out with the tweezers.

"Good. No blood. They were definitely ready to come out."

She worked her way from left to right, piling the stitches on a piece of gauze. She finished one stump and then the other. When she was done, she looked at Jack. "So, what do you think?"

Jack lifted his head. "You want my honest answer?"

Donna nodded.

"They're ugly. Sort of look like obese eels. Definitely not going to win any sexy-legs contest."

Donna laughed. "Well, the next step is seeing your prosthetist. He'll have you standing tall in no time at all on cutting-edge bionic legs."

Jack could hardly wait to show Pete his stumps. He rushed to the rehab gym in his wheelchair and found him setting up orange cones in the corner.

Pete waved, and Jack wheeled over to him as fast as he could.

"Today's the day!" Jack shouted.

Pete smiled. "Let's go see Lee and get that fitting."

The prosthetist measured Jack's stumps. "These look good, Jack. You'll start with stubbies. There's no knee component, just a socket sitting on top of a foot. Master those and we'll lengthen the pylon on the stubbies. We'll add knees to the prosthetic legs once your balance is good. Any questions?"

"Don't suppose I can skip the being-a-midget phase."

Lee shook his head. "Walking on stubbies is hard work. But believe me, it's much easier to get your balance than being way up high on full-length prosthetic legs with hinge-like knees. Right, Pete?"

"Right. Hopefully you'll only have your stubbies for a few days. That is, if you listen and do what I tell you."

"When do I ever not listen to you?" Jack joked.

Pete rolled his eyes.

"So when do you think I'll get them?" Jack asked Lee.

"I usually say twenty-four hours after getting casted. Figure on this time tomorrow coming in to try them on. You just keep working with Pete to increase your strength. A prosthesis is heavy. You're going to need a strong upper body in order to work them."

Jack and Pete headed for the rehab gym. They had a lot of work to do, and Jack planned to tackle it with renewed vigor. He hadn't realized what a monumental moment getting his stitches out would be. It meant progress. It meant he was closer to being at eye level with those standing around him. He hated looking up.

Zara started her morning with a run through a nearby park. She really didn't have the time, but she took it anyway. She always wanted to run a marathon, but her longest race was a 5K. Maybe that was another thing she'd concentrate on during her time in Florida.

She had rented a condo in Clearwater for six months. She figured that would be enough time to figure out her next move. Stacey, one of Zara's best friends, lived there and liked to run. Maybe they could do it together.

She ran the path that snaked through the park, past the kids' play area and sand volleyball courts. Past the pavilions with different bird names—Wren, Chickadee, Hummingbird, and others.

Running made her feel alive, and she could let her mind wander. Often, it was while running, when her mind was open to all possibilities, that a thought would pop into her head. That's what happened when she decided to move to Florida. The idea popped into her head when she hadn't been thinking about anything in particular but was struggling with Johnny's death and her growing feelings for Jack.

By the time she returned to her apartment, she was soaked with sweat but felt invigorated, ready to finish packing and moving on.

After showering, she tackled the kitchen. It was about the size of her mom's walk-in closet. She started with the top cabinets, wrapping the dishes and glasses in tissue paper before carefully stacking them inside a box. She picked up a French hand-painted roses saucer with scalloped edges. The antique teacup that belonged with the saucer had broken years before. Zara smiled, remembering what became known as "The Great Teacup Caper." Her mom was furious when she found the teacup, painted in 1893, in pieces on the floor.

Zara, not wanting to share her chocolates with Johnny, had hidden them in the teacup sitting high on one of the shelves. She hadn't realized Johnny was watching when she pulled the chair over to the bookcase, stood on it, and dropped her chocolate inside the teacup. Later when everyone was busy elsewhere in the house, the teacup fell to the floor and shattered. They found Johnny sitting on the floor, his hands and face covered in chocolate.

Tears gathered in the corners of Zara's eyes. Johnny wasn't the only one who'd gotten in trouble that day. To a six year old, it seemed so unfair. After all, Johnny was the one who'd broken the teacup.

"True," her mom had told her. "But you were the one who hid it there."

Zara ran her fingers over the saucer's scalloped edges. It occurred to her that life, like the French porcelain she held in her hands, was so fragile. One slip and it could shatter into a million pieces.

She carefully wrapped the saucer, using twice as much tissue paper than was necessary. But she didn't want anything to happen to the saucer. It was as much of a reminder about her past as it was about her future. Life, with all its moving pieces, could change in an instant. It was like a kaleidoscope, a quick turn of the cylinder produced something new, and it wasn't always as pretty as what came before.

She finished packing the items in her kitchen cabinets and was headed to her bedroom to remove the items in her closet when her mom called.

"Hi, Mom. No. Still packing. The movers should be here in a few hours. Yes, I promise I'll come and spend the night. I love you too."

She tackled her closet, putting the clothes she didn't want into a large plastic garbage bag she planned to donate to charity. She pulled out a gray cable sweater that had belonged to Johnny and rubbed it against her cheek. After he died, Zara went through Johnny's closet and took a few of his favorite sweaters. Wearing them made her feel closer to him.

She wondered if her mom had packed up his room yet. She'd offered to help, but her mom had snapped at her, telling her she wanted the room to stay just the way it was.

The last time Zara visited, everything was just how Johnny had left it. She knew her mom needed time and never brought it up again. But she'd check when she visited to see if anything had been changed or removed.

She finished her closet and looked at the clock. She had barely enough time to freshen up before the movers came to take everything to her storage unit. Shedding most of her stuff to live in a furnished condo felt liberating to Zara. She was beginning her journey without the weight of her past holding her down. She felt light, buoyant, and able to rise to the top of whatever she might face.

CHAPTER SIX

Twenty-four hours after getting casted, Jack tried out his new legs in the prosthetic department.

"How do they feel?" Lee asked.

Jack flashed a thumbs-up sign. "Man, I can't wait to run."

"Whoa," Pete said. "Slow down. You need to work on the basics first with your stubbies. That means building up your strength and working on your balance. It's definitely easier to balance on stubbies than on full-length legs. Plus, if you fall..."

"I don't plan on falling," Jack said.

"But if you do," Pete explained, "your risk of injury is less than if you fell while using standard prosthetic legs. Plus, walking on stubbies is just plain easier, so you'll be able to go faster."

"Pete's right," Lee said. "Master your stubbies. Work with Pete on balance and agility drills. They'll help build your confidence. You're going to have to learn to navigate everyday obstacles like curbs, stairs, and slopes. But if you practice, you'll get good at it and can progress to full-length legs with computerized knees."

By the time Pete and Jack returned to the rehab gym, Jack was ready to let lose. They headed for the parallel bars so Jack could try walking on his stubbies for the first time.

Jack grabbed the parallel bars and pulled himself upright. "Why'd you turn the feet around on these things?"

"It'll help you learn to balance. Plus, it'll help you clear the toe. And if you fall, you can catch yourself with your hands." Pete pulled out his cell phone. "Do you want me to videotape your first steps? Or take a photo?"

Jack had seen other patients celebrate their new legs with family members taking photos. It was usually a well-recorded celebratory event in the gym. He'd even seen videos on YouTube documenting the moment. But he didn't have any family, and he wasn't one for hoopla.

"Nah! I don't need a photo or video to remind me of this moment."

Pete put away his cell phone and knelt in front of Jack, moving backward as Jack moved forward taking one step at a time. Right step. Left step. Right step. Left step.

"Look ahead," Pete said. "Don't look down."

Jack lifted his head.

"Great. You're doing great. I know there's always a temptation to look down. Don't. Fight that. We want to establish good habits from the beginning."

When Jack reached the end of the parallel bars, Pete coached him on how to turn around.

"That's it. Nice and strong. How do you feel?"

"Tired," Jack said. Beads of sweat covered his face.

"You're doing great."

Jack continued. Right step. Left step. Head up. Eyes forward.

"Let's take a break," Pete suggested, helping Jack into his wheelchair.

Jack wiped the sweat off his face with a towel. Tears pooled in his eyes. "I never thought I'd walk again. I thought I'd taken my last steps in Afghanistan. I'm glad I was wrong."

Pete patted Jack's shoulder. "The first six to twelve months are the toughest. But we'll set goals. Realistic goals. Next, we'll turn your feet around. After the parallel bars, you'll use a walker and canes. As your balance improves, we'll lengthen your legs."

Jack smiled. "It sure will be nice to be six-foot-four again. And to run. How I want to run."

"If you want to run, you will," Pete said.

Jack took a sip of water. "What makes you so sure?"

"Because you want it so badly. Determination is the key. You can have the best prosthetic legs in the world, but if you aren't determined and don't work hard, they won't do you a darn bit of good."

"That's what Donna said."

"She's a smart lady," Pete said. "And a good nurse."

Jack pointed to a double amputee working with his physical therapist across the gym. "I remember watching him walk on his stubbies for the first time."

"And look at him now," Pete said. "Walking on full-length prosthetic legs. You'll get there, Jack."

Jack wasn't so sure, but when doubt tapped him on the shoulder, he remembered what Zara had written.

There's only one way for your dream to die and that's if you let it.

Man, he missed her. He even missed the citrusy scent of her hair. He wondered if she thought about him or if he had mistaken her kindness for something more.

Zara called Laura, and it went to voicemail. She figured Laura was probably in spinning class. Every Thursday, she met Jude after work for the killer session. The instructor was sixty-three and had two knee replacements but kicked everyone's butt. Zara left Laura a message, explaining the movers had come and gone, and she was on the road and planned to spend the night at her parents' house in Virginia before driving the rest of the way. She'd call Laura when she arrived in Florida.

Zara looked into the rear view mirror as she left Maryland behind. She'd seen so much in the last five years. Pain. Anger. Sorrow and death. But she'd also witnessed miracles—a quadruple amputee who'd walked. Amputees that went on to run marathons and do distance swimming. One even went skydiving. They were only limited by the differences between their natural limbs and prostheses.

Thoughts of Jack tiptoed into Zara's mind during the quiet moments of the day. She wondered how he was doing. Whether his stitches had been removed or if he was walking on stubbies. She knew he'd been close to that when she left, and she regretted not being there to celebrate the moment with him.

She missed his boyish smile. His dark hair, and dark eyes, and the way he scratched his head when he was nervous.

She wondered what his story was, how he ended up in the Marines. Everyone had a story. Some followed their fathers and grandfathers, becoming Marines and carrying on the family legacy. Some ended up in the Army because they had nowhere else to go. She figured Jack probably fell in with the last bunch. And if he had nowhere to go then, where would he go now, she wondered.

As the miles fell behind her, Zara questioned her decision. She knew where she was going, but somehow she thought she was probably just as lost as Jack. Her mind drifted back to the smiley-face pill puzzle, trying to get all those little balls into the right holes.

She pulled off the highway to get gas and heard the peals of a nearby church bell. It tugged on her heart in a way she hadn't expected, and she had the sudden urge to check out the church from which the sound originated. It was the weirdest thing, she thought. She hadn't been to church in years. Why did she suddenly find it so important to go to this church? She wasn't superstitious, but she couldn't ignore the urge she felt. So she asked the cashier for directions to the church and headed that way.

The church reminded her of the one she'd attended growing up—simple yet beautiful. Red brick, with a red door and a white wooden steeple topped by a spire that poked the sky. A middle-aged woman greeted her at the door and handed her a stone about the size of a quarter.

Zara looked at the tan nugget. "What's this for?"

"Just hold onto it, honey." The woman patted Zara's back. "It's part of tonight's sermon."

Zara slid into a wooden pew near the back of the church. She knew most people had their regular seats and didn't want to upset anyone's routine. Back home, her family sat in the same pew her mother's family had sat in for more than a hundred years. Her great-grandfather's suspenders had left scratches on the back of the pew where he had sat for the better part of his eighty-three years.

The inside of the church felt just as familiar as the outside. Red carpet, beautiful stained-glass windows, and wooden pews with racks on the backs that held the hymnals, Communion and visitor cards, and mini pencils. Zara always wondered why they put eraser-less pencils in pews. Church ought to be one place a person could erase a mistake, she thought.

Zara listened as the minister, bald with glasses and a warm smile, talked about the ripples each person caused in life.

"Every decision you make has a ripple effect on your life as well as the lives of others. Your choices are telling. What you want, love, and think are reflected in the choices you make. Just as Paul urged, make excellent choices."

As Zara listened to the sermon, a sense of peace filled her. She felt as if the minister was talking to her, even though there were at least fifty other people in the sanctuary for the Saturday night service. She couldn't get past the notion that she was meant to find this church and hear this sermon. It was especially startling because of the heart-shaped stone she'd found and its connection to Johnny and Jack.

Zara thought about the metaphor, how when people cast a stone into the water it created concentric circles rippling outward. The pastor had referred to it as "The Ripple Effect," an expanding series of effects or consequences that are the result of a single event or action.

After the closing hymn, the pastor invited everyone to come forward and drop their stone into a plastic kiddie pool. Zara clutched her stone and walked to the front. She waited as those in front of her dropped their stones into the pool and watched the concentric ridges of water expand outward. Zara was torn. She wanted to drop the stone into the water, and she wanted to keep it as a reminder. But then a thought sparked in her mind, and she dropped the stone, watching the ripples it created.

CHAPTER SEVEN

Jack sat on the mat in the rehab gym, rolling his silicone liners over his stumps. The liners provided some padding and protected his stumps from the hard plastic sockets. Pete helped him put on his stubbies.

"How do they feel?" Pete asked. "Are they snug enough?"

"I think I need to add another sock."

Pete handed him two more cotton-ply socks, and Jack put them on.

"Is the socket still too loose?" Pete asked.

"No, feels good. Will I ever see the day when I won't have to put on and take off these darn socks every half hour?"

"Yes." Pete explained, "The swelling will go down, and your stumps will shrink over time. Like Lee told you, you might go through a half-dozen temporary sockets before your stumps reach a stable size."

Jack stood and grabbed the parallel bars. He walked to the end, turned around, and walked in the other direction.

"You're doing great," Pete said. "You're improving all the time."

"I really want to push myself," Jack said.

Pete nodded. "Pushing yourself is good, but don't overdo it. You don't want to irritate your stumps. They can only take so much pressure, sweat, and twisting of the socket."

Jack paused.

"Everything okay?" Pete asked.

"I think I need to take off one of the socks."

Jack sat down and removed a sock from each stump. He worked on the parallel bars some more before Pete insisted they do some strength training.

"The stronger you are, the better you'll be able to control your prosthetic legs."

Jack watched as a new amputee was wheeled into the rehab gym in a cardiac chair. Lines and tubes draped across him. He remembered his first day in the gym, when he thought he'd never walk again. And here he was, walking on stubbies. He had a long way to go, but he was determined to get there.

Jack made it a point to welcome the newbie. On his way back to his room, he wheeled next to him. "Hi. Welcome to the rehab gym."

The guy, an above-knee, double amputee like Jack, clenched his teeth. "Screw you! This is the last place I want to be."

Jack nodded and wheeled himself away. He understood the soldier's anger, and he realized his own anger had lessened. He still had his moments, but he was beginning to accept the loss of his legs and realize that losing them didn't mean his life was over.

By the time Jack returned to his room, he was exhausted. He felt good about the progress he'd made with his stubbies. And he liked Pete. As frustrated as Pete made him at times, he knew Pete pushed him because he cared.

Growing up, there weren't a lot of people who had cared about Jack. But there were a few that stuck in his mind. Like Mr. Plato, his math teacher. Jack had trouble learning his times tables, and he worked with him after school. Jack walked to school, so he didn't have to worry about missing the bus. His mom, who worked two jobs, never came home before nine, so it wasn't like he had to rush home for dinner.

Most nights, he ate soup from the can or a peanut butter and jelly sandwich. If he was really lucky, which wasn't too often, his mom might throw a roast with potatoes and carrots in the slow cooker. But, yes, Mr. Plato had definitely made a difference in Jack's life.

And then there was the time he went to pay for his school lunch only to learn he had a zero balance in his account. His mom, who had promised to deposit money the night before, had forgotten. The cashier wasn't too happy, especially since she allowed him an IOU the day before. But the girl behind him handed the cashier her student ID to scan and said she'd pay for his lunch. He'd never forgotten that. And when she was on the homecoming court, he voted for her. He wasn't surprised she'd won.

Jack wondered if he'd made a difference in anyone's life. Maybe Nate's. Thinking of Nate reminded him of their last long conversation. One night when the drinking was heavy and the talk turned serious, Nate asked Jack to look in on his wife, who was expecting their first child, should anything happen to him. Then he'd handed Jack a gold four-leaf clover.

"But that's your good luck charm," Jack said.

Nate had told Jack he'd found the charm in an old cigar box stashed in his dad's dresser after his dad had died.

"My kid needs it more than me," Nate said. "And if something happens to me, I want to make sure he or she gets it."

"Nothing's going to happen to you," Jack had told him. "I'll die before you."

"You're too ugly to die," Nate teased. "But, man, seriously. I'm betting on you making it. Out of everyone here, you'll be the one who gets out of here in one piece."

It wasn't long after that the explosion occurred.

Jack wasn't a superstitious man, but he wondered if Nate had kept the charm if he'd still be alive.

When Zara walked into her parents' home, it was almost midnight. She found her mom asleep on the couch. She shook her arm. "I'm home, Mom."

Her mom stirred, and Zara shook her arm again. "Mom, it's late. I'm going to bed. I'll see you in the morning."

"Zara, sweetie. Is that you?"

"Yeah, Mom. I'm home. It's almost midnight. We'll talk in the morning."

Zara went to her room and turned on the light. She smiled. The room was exactly how she'd left it when she went away to college. Her field hockey and basketball trophies lined the white bookshelf. Photos of her and her high school friends crowded the dresser. Band posters hung on the pale pink walls. She sighed. It felt good to be home.

Funny, she thought. *When I was young, I couldn't get away from home fast enough. Now that I'm older, I've come to understand the value of what I left behind. There's a lot of truth to the saying, "Home is where your heart is."*

She planned to check out Johnny's room in the morning. She'd wondered if her mom had touched his room or if it too was just like he'd left it. In some strange way, she hoped everything was the same. She knew she'd find it comforting, just as she found her room to be. But she also knew how important it was to move on and live life.

Johnny wasn't coming home. He was buried in the cemetery down the street, the same one they'd played in as kids. She closed her eyes and pictured them flying down the hill, far away from the graves, on their sleds. That same hill was where Johnny was buried.

Through the years, the tombstones had taken over the land. It was no longer a place where kids could go. Except Johnny. He had a permanent place on that hill.

Zara crawled into bed, and sleep came quickly. She woke up to the smell of bacon frying in the kitchen. Every morning, her dad ate bacon and eggs, just as his dad had done before him. Zara's grandfather died in an accident when she was ten. It was the first loved one she'd lost. The last was Johnny.

She stumbled downstairs to find her parents in the kitchen, her mom at one end of the table, her dad at the other.

"Good morning, Princess." Her dad smiled.

Zara walked over, and her dad stood and squeezed her so tightly she coughed. "How's my little girl today?"

Zara yawned. "Sleepy."

"What time was it when you pulled in?" her mom asked.

Zara walked over and hugged her. "Around midnight. I made an unexpected stop, and the traffic was heavy. Sorry for keeping you up so late."

Zara's mom pushed out her chair. "Do you want me to make you eggs?"

Zara held up her hand. "No, sit. I'm just going to get some cereal." She walked over to the cabinet where the cereal was kept and opened the door. "No cereal?"

"Oh, forgot. I moved it." Her mom stood. "I reorganized the kitchen and switched some things."

Zara's mom showed her where she'd moved the cereal—and the bowls, and spoons, and coffee mugs. It bothered Zara that things weren't where she thought they'd be. She liked knowing what to expect when she opened a door.

Zara poured Lucky Charms into a bowl. She knew her mom bought it just for her. When she and Johnny were little, they'd save all of the marshmallows and eat them last. She liked the rainbows the best. Johnny liked the pots of gold.

Zara sat down next to her dad, who looked up from reading the morning newspaper. "You know, when I was a kid, there were only four types of marshmallows. Pink hearts, yellow moons, orange stars, and green clovers."

Zara smiled. "Always the walking Wikipedia, Dad."

He winked. "Are they still magically delicious?"

Zara nodded.

Her dad folded the paper and topped off his coffee. "So, tell me what you're thinking."

"That I need a manicure."

Her mom cleared her throat. "Zara, that's not what your father is talking about."

Zara sighed. "I know. I know. But it's complicated."

"I'm not going anywhere," her dad said. "Take your time."

"I just need time to figure things out."

"And you felt like you needed to quit the great job you had and worked so hard to get to figure things out?" her mom asked.

"Mom, don't start."

Zara's dad glared at her mom. "Maggie, stop. We said we weren't going to fight with Zara about this."

Zara set down her spoon. "Look, guys. I know you don't understand me. I know you think what I'm doing is wrong."

Zara's dad held up his hand. "I wouldn't say wrong, honey. Maybe a little extreme."

"Whatever. But it's something I have to do. Yes, I worked hard to become a nurse. Yes, it was a rewarding job. But I completed my commitment, and now I'm reassessing what I want to do with the rest of my life."

Zara looked at her parents, who remained silent and perfectly still. The awkward silence nudged her to keep talking.

"Working with all of those wounded soldiers. They reminded me so much of Johnny. They went in the service filled with so much hope and passion and came home so broken. And some, like

Johnny, didn't make it. Do you know how many nights I've spent feeling helpless, knowing that despite my best care and effort, I couldn't save my patients from their mental demons? Their screams. Their cries. The horrible look on their faces when they woke up to learn they'd never feel the grass tickle their toes. I'm tired. Beaten. I need to figure out my purpose in life, what I'm meant to be and do."

Zara didn't tell them about Jack. That he too was part of her reason for leaving. Instead, she crumbled into a sobbing mess. Her mom retrieved a box of tissues, and her dad took her hand in his.

"Zara, I had no idea you'd taken Johnny's death so hard," her mom said. "I'm sorry I've been so tough on you."

"Yes, sweetie," her dad said. "It's your life. Not your mother's or mine. Yours. And only you can decide the path it takes."

Zara blew her nose into a tissue. "Thanks, guys. I needed to hear that. Just like you reorganized the kitchen, Mom, I'm going to work on reorganizing my life."

CHAPTER EIGHT

"Look at you!" Pete punched the air. "Walking with canes."

Jack had quickly left the parallel bars behind and was walking with his stubbies, using two canes to help him balance.

Jack stopped to catch his breath. "How long do you think I'll be in my stubbies?"

"At the rate you're going, not long," Pete said. "I'll want to see you wearing them about six hours a day. You'll need to be able to walk on uneven surfaces and step on and off curbs. Master your stubbies. That's your goal. Then we move onto full-length prosthetic legs. Believe me, balancing on two artificial knees and two artificial ankles is tough. Most guys say it feels like they're walking on stilts."

Pete motioned for Jack to come over to the mat. "Let's take a break."

Jack wiped the sweat off his face with the towel Pete had given him. "Do you have someone special, Pete?"

Pete's eyes widened. "That's a question out of the blue."

Jack shrugged.

"Does my dog count?" Pete joked.

Jack laughed. "I had a dog once. His name was Bullet. He was a stray. I found him rooting through our garbage one day and brought him in the house. He looked like he needed a friend—and some food. My mom wasn't home, and by the time she'd figured out it wasn't me who had eaten all the leftovers, Bullet had become my best friend."

Pete smiled. "Dogs are great, aren't they? They love you unconditionally."

Jack took a sip of Gatorade. "So what do you know about Zara?"

Pete shook his head. "Give me a transition, Jack. You go from talking about your dog to asking about Zara."

Jack laughed. "Sorry. I've just been thinking about her since she left."

"Well, I don't know much." He pointed across the room. "She dated Chris for a while."

Jack looked in the direction Pete pointed. "The tall, bald-headed guy working with the girl on the mat?"

Pete nodded. "But that was a while ago. He's married now to this hot chick who works in HR."

"So that's it? You got nothing else?"

Pete shrugged. "Sorry. But if I hear anything, I'll let you know. Now, break's over."

Using his canes for support, Jack pulled himself up. They did some more exercises before he headed back to his room, insisting that he keep his stubbies on.

An hour later, Tom knocked and walked into Jack's room. "So I hear you're doing well."

Jack looked up from his iPad. "Hi, Tom."

Tom sat in a chair next to Jack. "Reading anything interesting?"

Jack ran his fingers through his hair. "I was reading about these guys like me who climbed Mount Kilimanjaro."

Tom smiled. "Oh, the Warfighter Sports Challenge. Those guys who do those extreme events are tough."

Tell me about it," Jack said. "I can't imagine a twenty-six-mile desert run or a one-hundred-mile bike ride."

"You don't have to just imagine it," Tom said. "You can do it if you want."

"You really think I could hike the highest peak in Africa?"

"Why not? I've seen a lot of guys who've participated in these extreme programs do things they never thought they'd be able to do. I know a double amputee that went skydiving."

Jack mashed his lips together.

"You see, Jack," Tom said. "It's not about your disability—it's about your ability. It won't do you a darn bit of good looking back over your shoulder at what you once were able to do. You've got to look forward. Make new plans. Set new goals."

Jack nodded. "Hey, I heard you're going to be a dad. Congratulations."

Tom smiled. "Yeah. It's a boy. We're naming him Nathan after my dad. We'll call him Nate for short."

Jack's eyes turned glassy. "That's a great name. My best friend's name was Nate. He was a gunner."

Tom arched his eyebrow. "Was?"

Jack sniffed. "He died in the explosion that ripped off my legs. Damn Taliban and their damn bombs."

Tom nodded and pulled the chair in the corner closer to the bed and sat down.

"How do you feel about what happened to Nate?"

"How do you think I feel? He was my best friend. He was married and had a kid on the way. Just like you. I should've seen the bomb. It was my fault."

Tom shook his head. "You know that's not true, Jack."

"A couple of days before the explosion, he gave me his four-leaf clover good luck charm," Jack explained. "He said if anything happened to him, I was to give it to his kid. Sometimes I wonder what would've happened if he'd kept the charm. Maybe he'd still be alive."

Zara walked into Johnny's room. Just as she'd expected, nothing had been touched since Johnny had last closed the door.

She walked over to his dresser and picked up his baseball glove. She slid her hand into the well-oiled glove, lifting it to inhale a combination of leather, dirt, grass, and sweat. For a few seconds, she was transported back in time, sitting in the stands and cheering for Johnny, who played first base.

She put the glove down and picked up his blue piggy bank, the one he'd received as an infant. She had a pink one made for her by the same woman in their church. With the tip of her index finger, she traced his birth date on the side.

She still remembered the day her parents brought him home. She was four, and she'd wanted a baby sister. She wasn't happy when she learned she had a brother. She laughed at the memory of dressing Johnny in her blue princess dress.

He was such a good sport. Even when he was older, Zara could talk him into doing things he'd rather not. Like the time she'd persuaded him to cover for her when she stayed out later than she was supposed to. Her parents were asleep when she got home from the after-prom party. When they questioned her the following day, Johnny vouched for her.

She owed Johnny so much, and she felt terrible she wasn't always nice to him. Like the time she'd convinced him he'd been adopted. He was only seven, and her revelation made him act out. Finally, one day he confronted their mom, who immediately retrieved his birth certificate from the safe to prove his sister wrong. Zara was grounded for that.

Zara sat on Johnny's bed. She smiled, remembering the time she came home early and found him and his first girlfriend kissing in his room.

She opened the nightstand drawer and found a purple bag that once held a bottle of whiskey. It was one of the many her dad had given her and Johnny over the years. Her mom wasn't happy that Zara's dad gave them the bags.

"What will the other parents think?" her mother had said.

"That we have good taste," her dad joked.

Zara filled her bags with Barbie clothes and jewelry. Johnny filled his with tiny metal cars and marbles. And green plastic Army men. He probably had more men in his army than the actual Army, Zara thought. Only Johnny's men never died. They were just stuffed into the purple bag to play with another day.

Zara opened the purple pouch and dumped its content onto the bed. It was Johnny's rock collection. Big ones. Small ones. Smooth ones. Rough ones. And there in the middle, the smooth, black heart-shaped rock he'd found on the riverbank so many years ago.

She picked it up and turned it over and over in the palm of her hand. The memory of that sunny day at the river was so thick she could wipe it from her brow. She could hear Johnny shouting, see his triumphant smile. A person would've thought he'd found a diamond that day. Zara stuffed the stone into her jeans pocket and returned the rest to the bag, which she'd decided to take with her.

Zara's mom walked in. "I just can't bring myself to change a thing in his room."

"I know, Mom." Zara's chin trembled as she tried to hold back the tears. "It's hard letting go. Sometimes I'll think I see him at the mall or movies. A guy will look like Johnny from the back, and my heart will skip a few beats. But when he turns around, it's never Johnny."

Zara's mom walked over and sat down beside her. She pointed to the bag. "What's that you found?"

[54]

"One of Dad's Crown Royal bags," Zara said. "This one's filled with stones."

Her mom smiled. "Johnny and his darn stones. I used to find them all over the house."

Zara bit her lip, weighing whether to share the stone sermon.

"Do you know why I was so late getting home the other night?" Zara asked.

Her mom shrugged. "You said the traffic was heavy."

"It was, but I also went to church."

Her mom took her hand. "Tell me about it."

She told her about stopping for gas, hearing the church bells, and ending up listening to a sermon about stones.

"It was the oddest thing, Mom. I felt like the minister was talking directly to me. And then when he invited us to drop our stones into the pool and witness the ripples it created, a crazy idea flew into my head. What if I handed out stones? What if I created an organization that recognized people for the positive ripples they've created? Maybe I'll call it Cause a Ripple. Recognize everyday folks who are making a difference. The cashier in the medical center's cafeteria who wears a smile like it's a piece of clothing. The Red Cross volunteer who brings magazines and candy for the wounded soldiers. The physical therapist that encourages the new amputee to get out of bed."

Zara hadn't realized she'd been holding her breath until her mom hugged her. "I think it's a wonderful idea, Zara. Not exactly sure how you're going to pull it all off, but I know you, and you'll find a way."

Her mom pointed to the bag of stones. "That's a bit odd. I mean, Johnny had tons of those bags filled with all sorts of stuff. Remember those Army men he was forever playing with? And those rubber balls he'd always buy for a quarter at the grocery store? All stuffed in those bags. He probably had a couple dozen stuffed with toys, and yet you found the one containing stones."

"So?"

"So, maybe it's a sign." Her mom patted her back. "Maybe you were supposed to find the stones. Maybe Johnny's trying to tell you something."

Zara couldn't hold back her tears. She sobbed, soaking her mom's shoulder. She couldn't remember the last time her mom held her so tightly, or the last time she'd cried so much. She hadn't realized how firmly she'd been holding on to Johnny's death until she started to loosen her fingers.

CHAPTER NINE

Jack woke up. His sheets were drenched in sweat. He dreamt he was driving a vehicle in the shape of a four-leaf clover and a bomb exploded underneath. He flew through the air and landed in a puddle of blood. He looked down at his legs. They were gone.

His eardrums hurt from the blast. Fires erupted, and shrapnel scattered. He watched Nate bleed to death. The top half of his body was on the ground. The lower half was in the vehicle.

"Jack." The nurse shook his arm. "It's okay."

Jack peeled back his eyelids, and the nurse helped him sit up. He let out a deep sigh and ran his fingers through his hair. "Damn! It always feels so real. Like I'm back in that hellhole."

The nurse held out a glass. "Would you like some water?"

Jack shook his head and took a deep breath, filling his lungs with air and exhaling it slowly. He continued this, focusing on his chest filling with air and then releasing it through his mouth. Eventually, he lay back down and the nurse left. But Jack tossed and turned the rest of the night. He was afraid to close his eyes, afraid to dream again.

He wished Zara had been on duty. Somehow, she was able to calm him whenever he had nightmares. Just her touch seemed to make his heart stop thumping as if it were going to pop out of his chest.

Maybe Zara was right. Maybe he should keep a journal. He wasn't much of a writer, but Zara told him journaling might help him cope with the trauma. She said it worked for other wounded vets—maybe it'd help him. She'd even bought him a black journal and a pack of pens.

"If you're like me," Zara had said, "I'm always losing my pens."

At the time, journaling was the last thing Jack wanted to do, but maybe he'd give it a try. It couldn't hurt.

When Jack walked into the gym that morning, Pete was working with another amputee. Jack sat on a mat and watched as Pete guided the vet, who was learning to walk on computerized knees, through a series of cone drills. The next thing Jack knew, he was being awakened by Pete. He'd fallen asleep on the mat.

"Rough night, eh?" Pete asked.

Jack sat up. "Yeah. Rough one."

"Are you up for this?" Pete asked.

Jack nodded. "Definitely! I want my knees, like the guy you were working with."

"Then let's get to work."

They started at the parallel bars but quickly moved on, stepping on and off boxes, tackling uneven surfaces, and any other challenges Pete could throw at him. "Fall down and get back up," Pete said.

Jack scrunched his face. "Why would I purposely fall?"

"Because," Pete held up his finger, "you need to learn how to get back up on your own. Let's face it, everyone falls. It's part of walking. Think of babies learning to walk. No different. They fall a lot. You'll fall too. So you need to learn how to fall to minimize injury to your body and your prosthetic legs."

Jack practiced what Pete instructed over and over. Then Pete led him through a series of balance and agility drills. Jack pointed to a woman who made walking with prosthetic legs seem simple. "How'd she get so good?"

Pete looked in the direction Jack had pointed. "Shonna? Shonna got good because she worked hard. She doesn't just wear her prostheses a couple of hours a day during physical therapy. They've become part of her daily life. In order to become independent on a pair of prosthetic legs, you have to do the same. And when you're at home, don't rely on a wheelchair. If you're not wearing your prostheses, don't use a wheelchair to get around the house. Instead, crawl and climb. Use your upper body and residual limbs to help you get where you want to go. Not only will this burn calories, but it will also tone your upper body and strengthen your residual limbs."

"You make it sound so easy," Jack said.

Pete smiled. "I know it's not. A double amputee works 300 percent harder than a person with two legs. But exercise and physical therapy will make you stronger and your body more flexible. And if you start eating better like I've told you to, a healthier diet will help too."

Jack headed back to the curb-sized boxes, stepping up and down. "You're doing great, Jack," Pete said. "How do you feel?"

Jack clenched his teeth. "Determined."

Zara decided to visit Johnny's grave before she left for Florida. As she walked down the familiar sidewalk, visions of her childhood flashed before her eyes. Riding her green bicycle with training wheels. Roller-skating on the uneven pavement. Falling and skinning her knees. In some strange way, nothing had changed and yet everything had changed. Her playmates had all moved away. Most of their parents had too.

And Johnny was dead.

Zara walked up the stone steps to Johnny's grave. Along the way, she passed graves of others she knew. Mrs. Kissel. Her first-grade teacher, Mrs. Marshal. Doc Herrold and old Mrs. Shue. The cemetery was filled with ghosts from her past.

She saw Johnny's grave from forty yards away. It was the most decorated one in the cemetery, thanks to Zara's mom, who insisted on blanketing it with a mountain of flowers. Zara knelt in front of the black granite stone. She ran her fingers over the words etched on the surface. *Deeply missed. Forever loved.*

Zara kissed her fingertips then touched the stone. "I miss you, Johnny," she whispered. "I brought you something." She dug into her jeans pocket and pulled out the smooth, black heart-shaped stone. She laid it on the base of the headstone. "I love you, little brother. Save me a spot next to you in Heaven."

Zara stood and scanned the cemetery. It seemed like every time she visited Johnny, there were more graves.

An hour later, Zara pulled out of her parents' driveway, waving goodbye. She headed for the Interstate and reached for the audiobook she'd bought for the trip and slipped it into her CD player. She had read the book numerous times since Stacey had suggested it. Zara had highlighted the important parts and would skim those from time to time. The inspirational book, written by Jack Canfield and Janet Switzer, talked about getting from where a person was to where he or she wanted to be. She was thankful Stacey had told her about the book.

She'd met Stacey at a bookstore. Zara had been scanning the crowded shelves of self-help books when Stacey walked up and pulled *The Success Principles* off the shelf.

"Is that good?" Zara had asked.

Stacey's eyes widened. "Very. It's my current bookstore book."

Zara pursed her lips. "Bookstore book?"

Stacey giggled. "I read it here." She dug a small red notebook out of her purse and waved it. "I record where I stop so I know where to start the next time I come."

"Why not just buy the book?" Zara asked.

"I would if I could, but I can't buy all of the books I want to read. So I buy some and read others here. Except, sometimes I end up buying a bookstore book because I liked it so much. I'm sure this will be one of those."

Zara smiled. "Do you come here often?"

"At least twice a week." She held out her hand to shake. "By the way, I'm Stacey."

Zara shook her hand. "Zara."

Zara pulled a copy of the book off the shelf and followed Stacey to the snack bar, where they bought frozen coffee drinks and huddled in a corner, sitting on heavy black leather chairs side by side.

Turned out, Stacey was a kindred spirit. She was impulsive, fun, and full of energy. Their friendship flourished as they clung to one another for support, navigating life's twists, and turns, and surprises. From that day on, they met weekly at the bookstore.

"You know," Zara had told Stacey one day, "There are some people you meet and you know right away you could be really good friends. Then there are others you meet and you just know you'll never be more than acquaintances. You're the former."

Zara missed Stacey. She was one of the reasons Zara had decided to rent a condo in Florida. Stacey, a journalist, had taken a job at a newspaper there, and when Zara visited her last winter, she fell in love with the warmth and sunshine. So she figured she'd rent there, spend time with Stacey, and figure out her next move.

As she drove, she listened to the narrator talk about a person taking responsibility for his or her life. He said those who succeed are those who believe they can.

It'd been a long time since Zara felt so energized by what she heard. She was taking responsibility for her life. With each passing mile, she became more excited about her stone idea. She knew she had a long road ahead of her, but she hadn't felt this sure about anything in a long time.

Zara pulled into a rest area to use the bathroom. She called her mom to check in and then Stacey. She noticed an older couple, with a small dog, eating sandwiches at a picnic table under a tall oak tree. The dog looked just like the wheaten Cairn terrier she and Johnny had growing up.

Johnny had begged for a dog, and her mom finally gave in, as long as it was small. Johnny named him Kakita after a Samurai warrior from his favorite role-playing game. He sure didn't remind Zara of a Samurai warrior. There wasn't a mean bone in his body. He was the most lovable dog Zara had ever met, planting sloppy, wet kisses on anyone who came close enough.

Kakita died six months after Johnny went into the service. Zara thought he probably died of a broken heart. Johnny never had a chance to say good-bye, but when they buried Johnny, they buried Kakita's ashes along with him.

Zara pulled back onto the highway, thinking about Johnny and how much she missed him. Tears filled her eyes. Even though they'd been close, they had their share of sibling fights growing up. But they always seemed to work them out.

"Unless there's bloodshed or something's broken, don't come get me," her dad would say. Looking back, Zara could see the value of her parents not interfering. She and Johnny learned to resolve their conflicts peacefully and to support each other. That love and support continued to grow as they aged.

Johnny was the one who found her crying in her room one night when she was in high school. Upset because she hadn't been chosen for the homecoming court and all of her friends had, she spent the evening comparing herself to them.

"Don't compare yourself to them," Johnny joked. "You'll never feel good about yourself. Compare yourself to the bag lady that lives in the cardboard box under the overpass."

Zara had hit his shoulder. "You're not helping."

"Look, Z," Johnny said. "There'll always be girls who are prettier and more popular, but you've got your own secret sauce that makes you super special. If you continue to compare yourself with others, you'll never feel good about who you are, and I think who you are is pretty great."

Zara bit her lip. "Think so?"

Johnny nodded. "I know so. Comparing yourself to others just confuses what really matters."

"How'd you get to be so smart?"

"Well, someone in the family had to get all of the brains."

Zara sniffed as she remembered the pillow fight that followed. Johnny had a knack for being able to turn her tears into laughter. She missed him. Why'd he have to enlist?

Zara turned the audiobook back on. The narrator talked about positive expectations, a person believing what they want is possible. Zara listened as he explained that most people failed to reach their goal because they don't believe they can. It reminded her of Laura and her positive self-talk. She started doing it about a year ago after seeing a therapist talk about it on TV.

"You ought to try it," she told Zara at the time. "You just repeat the statement throughout the day. I swear it'll change the way you think and feel."

Maybe Laura was right. Maybe Zara should try it. But she also knew a person couldn't just say affirmations and expect their life to get better. They needed to take the actions necessary to accomplish their goals. And she was.

By the time Zara had pulled into a hotel to spend the night, she'd listened to more than half the book. She'd finish it by the time she arrived in Clearwater the next day.

She couldn't wait to see the ocean.

Growing up, she and Johnny loved going to the beach. They'd build big sandcastles and dig huge holes to play in. Johnny was great at carving out steps leading down to their sand fort. She must have a hundred of those scopes the guys and girls in swimsuits peddled on the beach. Inside all of them was a photo of Johnny and her, arm in arm, grinning.

CHAPTER TEN

Jack woke up earlier than usual. He wanted to take a shot at journaling before he headed to the rehab gym. He retrieved the black notebook and the pens Zara had given him from his nightstand drawer. He ripped open the bag of pens and unlatched the journal, folding back the cover so it laid flat on the table. He felt awkward writing down his thoughts and emotions. At the same time, writing his innermost feelings without the fear of being judged was liberating.

"It helps you let go of negative thoughts," Zara had told him. "And there are physical benefits, such as enhancing your immune system and reducing your recovery time."

"Writing can do all that?" Jack had asked.

Zara nodded. "It helps get out what's on the inside. I keep one, and you'd be surprised how much of a de-stressor and mood-changer it can be."

Jack put his pen to paper.

I hate the Taliban, he wrote. *They killed my best friend and blew off my legs. If I could, I'd go back and kill every one of them.*

Jack wrote about two pages before closing his journal and stuffing it back inside his nightstand drawer. He ate some breakfast and made his way to the gym, where Pete and Lee, his prosthetist, were waiting for him. Jack walked over to them.

"You're really doing great on your stubbies," Lee said. "Ready to get a little taller?"

Jack grinned. "Are you serious?"

Lee nodded. "I think you're ready."

Lee added six inches and knee-like rotators to Jack's legs. "Remember, you have to get used to balancing."

"Are you telling me I'm top heavy?" Jack joked.

Lee smiled. "You have to learn to trust the knee. The new microprocessors have five sensors, compared with the original C-Leg, which had two. These babies can determine when you want to sit down or go upstairs, all without presetting the limb with a remote device."

"In other words, they're bionic." Jack laughed.

"Absolutely. In the old days, you had to swing your leg outward and project yourself forward to walk."

"Let's start on the parallel bars," Pete said.

Lee kneeled in front of Jack, adjusting the longer metal legs. "How does it feel to be standing up?" Lee asked.

"I feel tall," Jack said.

"You ready?" Pete asked.

Jack nodded. He took his first step. Then another. In short order, he was charging across the parallel bars.

"You're doing great!" Pete yelled.

Jack reached the end of the bars and twirled around. A big smile swallowed his face. "It feels great. I feel like the Bionic Man." His voice dropped. "Gentlemen, we can rebuild him. We have the technology. We have the capability to make the world's first bionic man."

Pete and Lee laughed.

Jack walked sideways in the parallel bars and then backward.

"What do you think?" Lee asked Pete.

"I think he's ready to ditch the bars for a walker." Pete placed a walker in front of Jack. "Remember, keep your head up."

Pete tied a strap around Jack's chest while Lee sat in front of him and made more adjustments to the legs.

Right step.

Left step.

Move the walker.

"Eyes forward!" Pete yelled. "Don't look down."

Step.

Step.

Move the walker.

The right prosthetic banged into the walker.

"Easy does it," Pete said. "You're doing great."

Step.

Step.

Move the walker.

Repeat.

It took Jack several minutes just to walk a few feet.

Sweat drenched Jack's face and neck. Pete handed him a towel. Jack wiped his face then draped the towel around his neck and continued.

"I must be burning a zillion calories," Jack said. "I can feel the sweat puddle up in the bottom of my sockets."

"Let's check your stumps," Pete said.

Jack sat down in a wheelchair and pulled off his prosthetic legs. He rolled the silicone liners off each stump, and sweat poured out of each one onto the floor. Pete looked at Jack's skin. It was pink and sweaty. "They look good," Pete said. "You're doing great."

Jack looked across the gym where a Marine with full prosthetics was strapped to a rail in the ceiling. The Solo Step ran the length of the room. He pointed. "That looks like fun."

Pete looked in the direction Jack had pointed. "Your turn's coming. See how there's just enough slack in the strap that if he falls it'll catch him before he hits the floor?"

Jack nodded.

"I've seen a guy ride a skateboard while being hooked up."

"Really?" Jack asked.

"Yep! If you want to do it, we'll help you achieve it."

Jack smiled, remembering all the videos he'd watched of double amputees like him snowboarding, skiing, hiking, rowing, and surfing. One guy he read about ran a marathon, something he hadn't done before he was injured. Jack was inspired by the tales of amputees overcoming their limitations. He wanted to be one of them.

Zara pulled up to the yellow stucco condo with plantation shutters and a tile roof. She turned off the car and sat for a minute, drinking in the scene. Tall palm trees and flowering shrubs. The pink hibiscus that hugged the corner of the condo was especially pretty.

Across the street were the clubhouse, pool, and gym. She was glad she'd paid extra to stay in a private, gated community. Maybe she'd meet some new people and make some new friends at the pool. And she loved the idea of getting back to exercising on a regular basis. She hoped to run every morning.

She opened the door and walked inside, finding the kitchen first. She ran her hands over the brown speckled counter tops. She loved the stainless steel appliances and cherry cabinetry. She moved into the great room with its vaulted ceiling and wall of windows. It was light and airy. The place was more luxurious than she'd expected.

She went down a short hallway to the master bedroom, located on the balcony side of the home. She sat down on the bed and bounced. It felt firm. She checked out the bathroom and imagined soaking in the big tub. Yes, she was going to love staying here.

She unloaded her stuff, making a dozen trips between her car and the condo. She was carrying in the last of her belongings when her neighbor pulled into the driveway next door. She looked to be about her grandmother's age, fashionably dressed in a yellow suit with black trim.

The woman walked over to Zara, who set down the box she was holding to extend her hand.

"Welcome to Cambridge Crossing," the woman said.

"Thanks. I'm Zara."

The woman smiled. "That's a lovely name. I'm Lilli. I'll let you get back to unpacking, but if you need anything, Mr. Horn and I are right next door."

Zara smiled. "Thank you. I did wonder where the closest grocery store was."

Lilli gave her directions. "It's only about five minutes from here. They have a good selection of meat and produce."

"I'll definitely check it out," Zara said. "Thank you for the warm welcome."

Lilli patted her shoulder. "Remember what I said. If you need anything, anything at all, we're right next door."

Zara picked up her box, and she and Lilli went into their homes. Just as Zara set the box on the kitchen table, her cell phone rang. It was Stacey.

"Hey, I got your text, but I was in a meeting," Stacey said. "You're finally here! I can't believe it. I'll come over after work. Probably around seven. I'll bring a pizza and a six-pack. Or would you rather have wine?"

"Beer is fine," Zara said. "See you later." Zara ended the call with Stacey, and her mom called. "I was going to call and let you know I got here okay, Mom. Honest."

"Yes, I won't forget to eat."

"Yes, I met the woman who lives next door. She looks to be about Grandma's age. Her name's Lilli. She told me where the closest grocery store is."

"No, I don't know if she golfs."

"I don't know if she reads either, or if she prefers steak over seafood, or shower gel over soap. Look, Mom. I just met her. We talked for five minutes."

"No, I'm not mad. Just annoyed. I hate when you ask a million questions."

"I love you too."

By the time Stacey arrived, Zara was pretty much settled in.

"I can't believe you're finally here," Stacey said. She put the pizza and six-pack on the table and hugged Zara. She scanned the kitchen. "This place is amazing. I can see why you didn't want to move into my dingy apartment."

"Your apartment's not dingy. I just wanted my own space. I hope you understand. Besides, you can stay over anytime you want. There's plenty of room."

Stacey cracked open a beer and handed it to Zara, who found plates in the cabinet next to the sink. They sat down and fell into easy conversation.

"So how are you really?" Stacey asked.

"Truthfully, a bit of a mess."

"Okay. I know that look. There's something more going on. What is it?"

Zara sniffed. "Where do I start?"

"From the beginning."

Zara told her about Jack, about how he scared her because she'd realized she was starting to have feelings for him.

"As much as I tried to stop myself from feeling for him, I couldn't. Just being near him made my heart flutter. I'd never been around anyone who made me feel that way. We had an instant connection. I felt it, and I think he did too. He's my patient, so that's a no-no."

"But you're both human," Stacey said. "I mean, you can't help who you fall for, right?"

"It's not quite that simple. One of the first things I learned is how to care but not become involved with a patient. You have to pinky-promise me you won't say anything to anyone."

"Of course." Stacey sipped her beer. "What about that runner who was injured in the Boston Marathon? Didn't he end up marrying his nurse?"

Zara nodded. She was a travel nurse who worked with him for several weeks while in rehab. Not that it makes any difference."

"Well, it seems silly."

"Think of it like this," Zara said. "It wouldn't be appropriate for you to write a story about me for your newspaper. We're friends. You might suggest the story to your boss, but you'd recuse yourself from writing it because of our relationship."

"True."

"And you wouldn't write a story about Tony opening another pizza shop, because Tony is your boyfriend. Again, you'd pass the information along to the business reporter but then stay out of it. There are certain boundaries."

"I can see not getting involved with a current patient, but months or years later when he's no longer your patient, I think it's silly to prohibit yourself from dating the guy if you're both interested in each other," Stacey said. "This, by the way, is exactly what happened to me and Tony. I interviewed him for a story, and months after the story, we ran into each other at a bar. He asked me out, and the rest is history."

"Yeah, but when he decided to open another pizza shop, you couldn't do the story."

"True," Stacey said. "Someone else had to. But it wasn't like the paper prohibited me from dating him because I met him through a work assignment."

"It was just starting to get too complicated," Zara said. "You know how you can look at someone and know there's more there?"

Stacey nodded.

"I'd look at Jack and I knew he could see it in my eyes. I saw it in his. I needed to leave so he could concentrate on getting well. And I knew that the time away would do me good. I have so much to figure out, including whether I want to stay in this profession or pursue something new."

"But I thought being a nurse was all you've ever wanted?"

Zara shrugged. "Maybe not anymore. People change. I've changed. Losing Johnny. My mess of a relationship with Chris, who I was never able to truly let into my heart. And meeting Jack and my growing feelings for a guy I could never have. I'm so messed up." She looked around. "I'm glad I'm here. I need time to figure out my life. And there's something new I'm working on."

Stacey pulled her legs up on the couch. "Oh, sounds mysterious. Do tell."

Zara started with finding the heart-shaped stone then proceeded to hearing the sermon and discovering the stones in Johnny's bedroom.

"Wow!" Stacey said. "Kind of creepy how this all came together. I mean, creepy in a good way."

"I know. And I'm not sure if it's because stones have been on my mind, but I swear I've seen them everywhere today. The stone entranceway, the planters made out of pebbles on my neighbor's porch, around the bushes, and trees at the clubhouse."

"Yeah, it's because it's top of mind. When I started dating Tony, I saw pizza everywhere. Commercials on TV. Pizza shop flyers in the break room. Banner ads on websites. Now I don't see them nearly as much, but I'm sure they're around."

"It feels so good to see you, Stace. I'm glad I came."

"Me too. And I'll help you with Cause a Ripple. Or put you in touch with someone who can."

"Thanks!" Zara got another beer and handed one to Stacey. They opened them at the same time. Zara held hers up. "To friendship and a new adventure. May we both find happiness and everything we're looking for in life."

CHAPTER ELEVEN

Over the next couple weeks, Jack's journeys around the medical center's hallways and indoor track lengthened, as did his legs. He continued to do a lot of sit-ups and side body lifts to build up his core strength.

"Ready to leave these smooth, polished floors and tackle the great outdoors?" Pete asked one morning.

"Bring it on." Jack followed Pete outside. The warm sunshine felt good on his face. He walked over pathways made of gravel, sand, concrete, and pavers. He walked up and down a ramp, over a bridge, and came to a large climbing wall that stretched high into the sky.

He watched a double amputee climb the wall. "I want to do that," he told Pete.

"Okay. Then we'll work on that."

Jack left the path and walked on the lumpy grass, catching himself when he tripped over a hole in the ground. He tackled the concrete plaza laced with brick interlays. Sweat poured off his face, and Pete handed him the bottle of water he'd brought along.

"Incredible," Pete said. "Great work."

"How many miles do you figure I've logged so far walking on my bionic legs?" Jack asked.

"Not sure," Pete said. "Probably hundreds." He pointed to Jack's prostheses. "Pretty neat how your computerized legs automatically adapt to the speed, length, and frequency of each step."

Jack nodded. "Yeah, especially when I'm walking on slopes or uneven surfaces. Weird how it feels like I'm walking in shoes tied too tight."

"Does the socket hurt?"

"No, it feels good."

They walked back inside and headed for the rehab gym, where Jack sat on a mat.

"Can I ask you something?" Pete said.

Jack nodded.

"That bracelet you're wearing. That's new, isn't it?"

Jack felt the paracord bracelet on his left wrist. "Yeah, I ordered it online, and it came the other day." Jack held out his arm so Pete could read the name and date etched on the bracelet. "It's my buddy who died and the date of the attack. I wear it in honor of his service."

Pete smiled. "Cool. Very cool, Jack. I'm sure your friend would be honored."

By the time Jack returned to his room, he felt exhausted. He wanted to write in his journal, something he'd done daily since starting several weeks ago, but decided to rest first. He fell asleep almost instantly but tossed and turned as he battled his nightmares. They'd become less frequent, but when they returned, they did so with a hurricane force that shook him to his core.

The blinding flashes.

Flying and flipping through the air.

On his back, his legs gone.

Blood everywhere.

Zara holding him as he cried into her shoulder. Her hand patting his back. Her voice telling him to breathe. "Breathe, Jack. Just breathe. I'm here. You're all right. You're safe."

Jack jerked awake, expecting to be in Zara's arms. But he was alone.

Damn Zara. Why'd she leave, he thought. *I know she felt something. But she left. Just like everyone else.*

His dad, who split before Jack was eating solid foods. The man never gave Jack anything but his lousy last name. "Screw him!" Jack punched the bed.

His mom, who deserved a life much better than the one she got.

And Nate.

They had all left him.

Jack could still see Nate lying several feet away, screaming in agony and then silent.

Damn Taliban. Jack punched the bed again. He was soaked. His sheets were soaked. He crawled out of bed, grabbed his journal, sat down at the table, and started to write.

I hate the Taliban.

I hate the Taliban.

I wish I could kill them all.

There was a knock on his door.

"Yeah?"

Sam, a Marine who had also transitioned to a small apartment on the medical center campus, opened the door. "You up for playing poker later?"

Jack nodded. "As long as you don't take all my money like the last time."

"I'll try to lose, how's that?" Sam flashed a toothy smile and walked closer. "Everything okay, man? You look like hell."

"Thanks," Jack said. "I feel like hell."

"Want to talk about it?"

[76]

Jack waved his hand. "Nah. Not now. Maybe later. I'm going to write."

Jack liked Sam. He reminded him of his shop teacher in high school, a bear of a guy with a gap-between-his-front-teeth smile and more hair than he could handle.

Sam left, and Jack returned to journaling. Instead of writing how much he hated the Taliban, he wrote about his day. About walking outside on his new legs, feeling the sun's warmth on his face, watching the Marine climb the rock wall. How he almost fell on the grass and the gorgeous girl he'd seen walking across the concrete plaza. Man, was she built. She looked all Hollywood with legs that went on forever and blowing-in-the-wind hair that fell down past her narrow shoulders. It had been a long time since he'd spent time with a girl.

He was in love once, but that was a long time ago. Becca had been his high school sweetheart, and he thought they'd be together forever. She said she'd wait for him to get out of the service, but halfway through her freshman year in college, she pledged a sorority and hooked up with a frat boy. That was the end of Jack.

He made a cup of coffee and wrote some more. This time, he wrote about Zara.

Within a few weeks, Zara settled into a routine. She ran in the mornings and swam in the evenings, spending her afternoons working on her stone project.

Cause a Ripple needed a logo and a website. She was over the moon when she'd discovered the domain name was available and purchased it.

Stacey had hooked Zara up with her friend Bobbi, a graphic designer at the newspaper who freelanced on the side. Zara asked Bobbi to design a logo and sent her images she found on the

Internet to give her an idea of what she had in mind. Bobbi was coming over later, along with Stacey, to show Zara what she'd come up with. And Zara had hoped to show them her choice of stones, if she settled on one by then.

Zara had spent weeks researching stones, trying to figure out what they should look like. White? Tan? Brown? Shiny or not? And size. How big should they be? She definitely didn't want them to be too small. They'd be a choking hazard if a child happened to pick it up.

She followed one link and then another and blinked when the perfect stone flashed on her screen. It was a black polished river stone. Zara gasped and instinctively touched the screen. It reminded her of the smooth, black heart-shaped stone Johnny had found. She checked the size chart. She could get it large enough that it wouldn't be a choking hazard.

The more she researched the stone, the more excited she became. She could get the phrase *Cause a Ripple* printed on the stones in gold lettering. She thought gold lettering on black would really stand out. She bookmarked the page so she could show Stacey and Bobbi when they arrived. Next, she'd have to figure out packaging.

Zara's phone rang. It was Stacey.

"We're on our way. Hope you don't mind, but Rob is coming along."

Zara gasped. "The reporter you wanted to fix me up with?"

"Uh, yeah."

Zara clenched her teeth. "I'm going to kill you. I look a mess."

"Well, he does too. He's been working all day. Besides, he doesn't know I invited him along to meet you. He thinks we're going to Rolo's afterward, which we weren't planning to do but will have to now."

"I am so going to kill you."

"But it was the only way to get him to come along without him knowing the real reason I wanted him to. Besides, you could use a drink or two. You've been really uptight. And Rolo's isn't far from your place. We'll be there in about fifteen minutes."

Zara hung up the phone and jumped into the shower. She towel dried her hair before applying mousse. She looked into the bathroom mirror and frowned. I look so pale, she thought. She reached for the basket she kept on the counter and grabbed her black vinyl makeup bag. By the time they pulled into the driveway, she looked more beautiful than she felt.

It's not like she had been interested in Rob, but Stacey insisted they meet. She said Rob would help her forget Jack. Zara wasn't so sure. A day hadn't passed that she didn't think about Jack. So she agreed to meet Rob sometime. She hadn't figured on sometime being so soon.

Rob drove in a separate vehicle and pulled in behind Stacey and Bobbi.

"Hi, everyone," Zara said. "Come on in."

Stacey hugged Zara. "Nice shower sprint," she whispered. "You look great!"

Stacey did the introductions, and Zara offered them a drink while Bobbi showed her what she'd come up with.

"See the concentric circles emanating out?" Bobbi asked. "It shows the impact of something hitting the water."

Zara studied the image. "I love it." She pointed to the upper right corner. "What do you think about adding a water lily there?"

Bobbi pursed her lips. "I like the idea of adding something there, but I'm afraid a colorful lily might take the eye away from the ripples. We want the ripples to be the focus. But maybe a green water fern. A few leaves peeking out of the top. Let me see what I can find, and I'll modify the image and e-mail it to you."

Zara showed them the stone she'd found. "So what do you think?"

"I like it," Stacey said. "And it looks big and flat enough that you'll be able to get Cause a Ripple printed on it."

Rob, who was given the cliff notes about Zara's project before leaving work, hadn't taken his eyes off her since arriving. "I think what you're doing is really neat," he said. "I could definitely see this keepsake being something people buy for others as a way to recognize the difference they've made."

Zara smiled. Rob got it. "Thanks. I hope so. I've been thinking about it for a long time. It's great to finally see it coming together."

Everyone finished their drinks and headed to Rolo's bar. Rob offered to take Zara, and she accepted. He seemed nice, and she was lonely. It would be great to have another friend.

On the drive to Rolo's, Zara learned Rob was originally from Pennsylvania but had attended college in Tampa and decided to stay after he graduated. He had interned at a newspaper there, and when they offered him a job after graduation, he couldn't turn it down.

"I hated the cold and snow," he said. "Going out in the morning to clean off my car when it snowed was the pits. I don't have to worry about that here."

"Yeah, but you have a lot more bugs down here, right?"

Rob nodded. "But I'd rather have bugs than snow and ice."

Stacey had already commandeered a high-top table by the time Zara and Rob arrived. Stacey bought the first round, and they settled into easy conversation.

Bobbi bounced back from the ladies room. "Guess what?" She didn't wait for a reply. "It's karaoke night."

Stacey looked at Zara.

"Oh, no." Zara shook her head. "There's no way you're going to get me up there. Remember the last time?"

"How could I forget?" Stacey said. "It was my going-away party, and you and Laura sang *Satisfaction*."

Rob laughed. "Love the Rolling Stones. Best guitar riff ever."

Bobbi and Stacey immediately launched into the chorus of *Satisfaction*.

Zara stood her ground about singing but watched as Bobbi, Stacey, and Rob took to the stage to sing *These Boots Are Made for Walkin'*.

Two hours later, they headed out the door. Rob insisted on taking Zara home. Their drive was filled with small talk about Rob's job and Zara's stones.

"I never really thought about how my actions and decisions affected others," Rob said. "I've always just done what I wanted to do."

"Most of us are like that," Zara said. "It's human nature, I think."

"But listening to you talk about the stones makes me feel like a schlep. Like maybe I should give my actions more thought." He stopped at the intersection, looking both ways before continuing.

"You make the best decision you can," Zara said. "Just like now. You could have turned right or you could have turned left. You chose to go straight because you're taking me home. That's an easy decision and an expected outcome. But a lot of the decisions we make affect others in ways we can't possibly know in advance.

"You smile at the senior citizen in line at the grocery store and chat her up, for example. What you don't know is how lonely she's been and how happy you've made her because you took the time to talk to her. Life is full of these moments—the expected and unexpected blend to create a picture of our life, filled with various colors and textures. A work of art."

Rob pulled into Zara's driveway. "You should be a writer."

Zara smiled. "I'll leave that to the pros like you and Stacey. But if you ever need someone to stitch a cut, you know where to find me."

Rob laughed. "I had a great time tonight."

"Me too," Zara said. "I'm glad Stacey talked me into going."

"I'm glad she did too."

Zara reached for the door handle. "Thanks for the ride, Rob."

"No problem. Maybe we can do it again sometime."

Zara smiled and climbed out of the car. She turned and waved before closing the door.

CHAPTER TWELVE

Jack looked at his hand and threw down his cards. "I'm done."

"Ah, come on," Sam said. "The night's young."

Jack yawned. "Not for me. Besides, you took enough of my money for one night."

Two of the other players called it a night too and headed back to their apartments. Sam and Jack stayed and had another beer.

"Do you ever get so crazy you just want to punch everyone?" Sam took a swig of beer.

Jack nodded.

"I miss my damn arm and my damn leg," Sam said. "I hate that I can't tie my damn shoes or open a damn jar of peanut butter."

"I'm thinking about training for a marathon," Jack said.

Sam shook his head. "I could never do that."

"Yes, you could. You've got one more leg than me."

"Yeah, but you have two arms."

Jack laughed. "Okay. We're both pretty messed up. But everyone has challenges. Our injuries are different, but they aren't excuses."

"What happy drink have you been guzzling?" Sam asked.

Jack held up his can of beer. "Just this and water. And energy drinks in the gym. But I've been watching a lot of videos of guys like us mountain climbing, skiing, running. Some of them are missing three, four limbs."

"Really?"

Jack nodded. "I'm not saying it's going to be easy. It's going to be hard. But these guys have overcome huge obstacles to achieve something great. They inspire me to try."

"I didn't even run when I had all my limbs," Sam said. "Maybe you can show me those videos sometime."

"Sure. And if you're not interested in running, there's always swimming or another adaptive sport. I even saw a guy snowboard. "

Jack left the lounge on the first floor of their building and returned to his apartment and reread what he'd written in his journal earlier. Not about the Taliban, but about Zara.

It seemed as if the more he tried to forget her the more he thought about her. He would've never guessed anything good would've come from losing his legs, but he had met her.

He still had his moments. His adrenaline spiked if a stranger passed too close behind him, and he always avoided crowds and sat with his back to the wall in restaurants. And earlier he'd stumbled on the carpet and fell.

The frustration he felt from not being able to do all of the things he used to be able to do caused him to launch verbal bombs that would surprise even the most foul-mouthed sailor. His actions always led to reactions of guilt and embarrassment.

There were veterans who had it far worse than he did. One guy he friended on Facebook was a quadriplegic, and it seemed to Jack that he spent most of his life trying to drink himself to death. And another he met online hadn't lost any limbs but was so depressed and drowning in post-traumatic stress that he was just as crippled as if he'd been blown up by a bomb or hit by a bullet.

Jack patted his prostheses, thankful for the mechanical legs with microprocessors that anticipated movement. He imagined what curved carbon-fiber prosthetics that allowed high-performance running would look like.

He liked what he'd imagined.

Zara called Laura as soon as she walked in her house.

"What's wrong?" Laura sounded anxious.

"Nothing."

"Don't tell me nothing. You wouldn't call this late if something wasn't bothering you."

Zara sighed. "You know me too well."

"So let's hear it," Laura said.

Zara told her about Rob. "He's attractive. He is. Sandy blonde hair and blue eyes."

"Definitely sounds swoon worthy."

"He is, but..."

"But what?"

"He's not Jack," Zara said.

Laura sighed. "Well, I did some checking like you'd asked me to."

"You were discreet, right?"

"Of course. Aren't I always discreet?"

"Do you really want me to answer that?" Zara asked.

"No. Anyway, I learned Jack is doing well. He's living in an apartment on the medical center campus and has his prostheses."

Zara smiled. "Good. Then he's making progress. So who's your informant? He has to be working on the inside."

Laura laughed. "I ran into Chris today. He asked about you, by the way. Anyway, I told him you'd wondered how your old patients were doing. I asked about the others too so it wouldn't be obvious you cared for Jack."

"Thanks."

"So how's it going? Ready to move back yet?" Laura asked.

Zara laughed. "It's only been a few weeks. I like it here. I'm a little lonely, but I like the weather, and there's a lot to do in the area. And, of course, Cause a Ripple is keeping me busy."

Zara had told Laura about the sermon and her plans to establish a stone ministry shortly after she'd moved to Florida.

"That was my next question," Laura said. "Have you settled on a stone yet? Or figured out the packaging?"

When Zara first got the idea of giving people stones in recognition of the positive impact they had on others, she'd considered collecting smooth river stones and painting them herself. However, she quickly dismissed that idea. She needed a company that could supply the stones in bulk.

"I did find a stone. It's gorgeous. Smooth, shiny, flat, and about two inches long."

"So big enough that the words Cause a Ripple will fit on it?"

"Definitely. And I can get the lettering in gold, which will be nice."

"And the packaging?" Laura asked.

"Still working on that. But the logo and website are all in the works."

"I can hear the excitement in your voice," Laura said. "I haven't heard that in months."

"Thanks. I haven't been this happy in a long time, and that scares me. It's like I'm waiting for something bad to happen. Things can't stay this good forever."

"Who says?" Laura asked. "They might get even better."

Zara finished talking to Laura and picked up *Pride and Prejudice*. She'd lost count of how many times she'd read the book. It fit like a glove in her hands. It was familiar. Comfortable. Worn and a bit tattered. But she loved it anyway. Something didn't have to be perfect to be loved, she thought.

She crawled into bed and picked up her iPad, reading an article she'd come across earlier in the day. The story said the secret to a person's happiness is to discover their gifts and share them with the world. Zara wondered what her gifts were. Maybe she didn't have any.

She did as the article suggested and made a list of the things she was passionate about. Then she made a second list of those things she was an expert in, or at least knew a lot about. The trick, according to the author, was to integrate what she was good at with what she wanted to do. The goal was to do what she loved and love what she did.

She was passionate about helping people. It's why she became a nurse. But were there other ways she could help people? She didn't have to give up nursing, but how else could she help?

She picked up the printout of the Cause a Ripple logo Bobbi had given to her. This had become her mission. She'd help people by recognizing their goodness. Maybe she could sell the stones for others to give as gifts and use the proceeds to make a difference by donating to various charities.

She'd been working on designing her website and had showed it to Stacey, Bobbi, and Rob earlier. Rob had made some suggestions and offered to help. Maybe she'd take him up on his offer. She'd have to integrate a shopping cart into her website and wasn't quite sure how to do that.

She thought about the audio book she'd listened to on the drive down to Florida. She tried to visualize success as she'd read in the book. Every time she visualized what success meant to her, she'd see a stone, black with gold lettering, sitting on desks, bookcases, and nightstands. Anywhere it could be seen, picked up, felt, and held. She wanted the stones to be an inspirational reminder of a person's lasting impact, of the positive ripples they'd created.

She wanted Cause a Ripple to grow into a tidal wave. She thought people were amazing and wonderful.

We need to notice and appreciate that.

CHAPTER THIRTEEN

Tom met Jack in the bar one night not long after he had the conversation with Sam about training for a marathon.

"So what do you think?" he asked Tom. "Think I'd be able to do it?"

Tom nodded. "I think if you want to, you will. It all comes down to determination and commitment. It's a great way to stay healthy. It works your upper body while keeping your heart rate up. And it strengthens your core. A buddy of mine got heavily involved in a program that trains wounded vets for races. A lot of them use hand-crank wheelchairs. It's sort of like a three-wheeled cycle powered by hand pedals."

"I've seen those," Jack said. "I watched a video of some guys competing in a New York marathon. They were amazing."

Tom sipped his beer. "I couldn't believe how great Jared got. And we're talking about a guy who had two collapsed lungs and could barely breathe at one point. He started out participating in short races, like five-milers, and eventually worked up to doing marathons. Now he participates in races all over the country. Boston. New York. LA."

"Does he use a hand-crank or run on artificial legs?"

"At first, he used the hand-crank. He did his first marathon using that. But eventually, he ran on artificial legs. The guy is amazing. I'll call him and see if he'd be willing to talk to you. I'm sure he will."

"Thanks," Jack said. He saw a blonde with curly hair out of the corner of his eye. For a second, his heart fluttered, but then he turned and realized it wasn't Zara.

"Pretty hot, huh?" Tom said.

Jack smiled. "At first, I thought she was someone else."

"Still thinking about her, eh?" Tom tossed some peanuts into his mouth.

Jack nodded. "Crazy, I know. It's not like I have a shot of ever seeing her again. But, man, I liked her."

"You never know," Tom said. "A month from now, a year, whatever, you might be doing something and you'll run into her unexpectedly. Life's weird like that."

"Can I ask you something personal?" Jack said.

Tom nodded.

"What's it like being with a girl when you have no legs?"

Tom smiled.

"What's so funny?"

Tom held up his hand. "Sorry. It's just that I'd expected you to ask sooner. I did. But that was probably because I had Jen and I was really worried what it would be like."

"Well? What's it like?"

Tom cleared his throat. "Different. At first, I didn't think Jen would want me. I mean, who'd want to be with a guy with no legs? But she was great. We talked a lot and took it slowly. At first, I was angry and compared my life to what it was in the past. But she made me see that my disability is part of who I am. It doesn't define me. Eventually, we figured it out."

Jack listened, allowing Tom's words to soak in. He knew he was lucky his man parts hadn't been damaged. One guy he'd met had lost one testicle and part of the other and had to take testosterone daily. Still, he worried about being intimate. What would it be like? What if he couldn't? Should he take his legs off or keep them on?

"So how do you like your new legs?" Tom asked.

Jack smiled. "Not as good as what I had, of course, but still pretty darn good." He breathed deeply and exhaled slowly, as if the extra seconds gave him time to weigh his words. "I still dream of having my real legs sometimes. I'll be playing baseball with my buddies, or hiking, or walking on the beach and I'll wake up to find that my legs are gone. I'd give anything to be able to dig my toes into the sand one more time. Stupid, I know. I mean, who'd think you'd miss digging your toes into the sand?"

Tom nodded. "Odd you mentioned the sand. I know one guy who was hit by a rocket-propelled grenade in Afghanistan. He lost his right leg and severely damaged his left. For months, they worked to save his leg, but he was in so much pain he asked them to amputate it."

"He actually had his leg and wanted it removed?"

Tom shifted in his seat. "It wouldn't heal, and he was in so much pain. He looked at those of us who came in at about the same time and were fitted with artificial legs. We were walking while he was still stuck in his wheelchair. I guess he saw the progress we were making and realized he'd be better off without it. But he went to the beach before they took it off. He'd grown up on the eastern shore and spent his childhood on the Delaware beaches. He wanted to feel the sand sift through his toes one last time."

Jack mashed his lips together. He'd never feel the sand sift through his toes ever again.

Zara had been stuck on figuring out how to package the stone. A box? A bag? A tin? She did lots of research, and the cost to create prototypes was crazy expensive. First, she wanted a box with a water ripple photo on top, but it cost too much to create just one to see what it would look like. Ditto for a wooden box with a burned-in logo on the top.

Next, she considered a leather bag with a burned-in logo, but she decided against that too. She was about to give up when she stumbled upon a small woven bag online. It was sturdy and tan, which gave it an earthy feel, something she liked.

She called Stacey. "I think I found something that might work."

"Uh, for what? Your bloated stomach you've been complaining about?"

Zara laughed. "No. I think I found a bag for the stone. I'll e-mail you the photo. Check it out and call me back."

Stacey called her right back. "I like it. Are you still planning to get the logo printed on cards?"

"Yes. I'll have to figure out how to attach the card to the bags. I'd like the stone to be visible so anyone picking up the bag can see what it's all about."

"It'll make a great keepsake," Stacey said.

"Precisely. Have you seen Bobbi's revised logo?"

"Yes," Stacey said. "And I like it a lot. The greenish blue color is so much better than the muddy version. And the fern you suggested she add to the top is perfect."

Zara explained how she wrote a poem and she hoped to fit it on the back of the card. "I found a company who can do a really thick business card with a silk finish and rounded corners. I just need to get Bobbi to configure the art file to fit the card's specs."

"It really sounds like things are starting to come together," Stacey said.

"I'm making progress, but I still have a long way to go. Rob's coming over later to help me with the website. I figured out most of it, but he's going to go over it and make sure it looks good."

Zara finished talking to Stacey and called Laura. She wanted to get her opinion too. "I just sent you the logo. What do you think?"

There was a pregnant pause while Laura grabbed her iPad.

"Love it," Laura said. "Especially the colors. Much better than the first image you sent."

"Yeah, I like how Bobbi made it greenish blue. And the font. What do you think about that?"

"I like it. It's clean. Easy to read."

"Great, then I'll order the cards. I wanted to run it by you first because I know you'll tell me if you think it's dumb."

Laura laughed. "I don't think anything you've ever done has been dumb."

"What about the time I..."

"Okay. You rarely do anything that's dumb."

They laughed.

"So how's Jude?"

"He's driving me crazy with house hunting. I swear he's taken me to see a dozen houses so far, and I haven't liked one of them. They all, of course, had gorgeous garages, but the kitchens and bathrooms were horrible. Too small and too outdated. Why is it that guys are so garage crazy anyway?"

Zara laughed. "I guess for the same reasons we love big bathrooms and colossal closets. Sounds like a compromise might be in your future."

"Meet anybody new?"

"Not really. But then, I'm not looking. Hear anything more about Jack?"

"I was wondering how long it would take you to ask about him."

"I'm just curious about a past patient," Zara said.

"Sure. Whatever you say. But I haven't heard anything more. I promise I'll let you know the moment I do."

Just as Zara got off the phone with Laura, her doorbell rang. Zara opened the door and waved Rob in. "Thanks for stopping over."

"No problem. I had an assignment nearby anyway."

By his clean-shaven face and a hint of manly musk aftershave, Zara figured he was probably lying. More likely, he had scrambled home after work and showered before coming over.

Zara offered him a beer, and she grabbed one for herself. They sat down at the dining room table, where Zara had set up her laptop.

Rob scrolled through her website. "It looks good. What do you think about adding your social share buttons here?" He pointed to the screen.

"I like that idea," Zara said. "I was thinking of creating a Pinterest board for Cause a Ripple. I could ask people to share photos of where they've displayed their stone and pin them to the board."

"Good idea," Rob said. "Make sure you link the pins to your website. So if someone clicks on the pin it will take them to the point of purchase. Might get more sales that way."

"Definitely," Zara said.

Rob turned to look at her. "Can I ask you something?"

Zara nodded.

"Are you dating anyone?"

She shook her head.

"Would you like to go out sometime?"

Zara wasn't sure what to say. She liked Rob, but she wasn't all fluttery inside when she was around him the way she was around Jack. And she wasn't certain she was in a good place mentally to date. "I'm not sure I'm great dating material right now. But I'd like to be friends if you're up for that."

Rob pouted. "You know you just broke my heart, right?"

Zara softly slapped his arm. "Now you're making fun of me."

Rob picked up his beer. "Seriously, it's okay. To friends!"

Zara picked up her beer bottle, and they clanked them together.

An hour later, they'd finished the website. "The only thing left is to upload the product shots," Rob said.

"I should be able to do that in a couple of weeks," Zara said. "The stones, bags, and cards should be here by then."

Zara closed her laptop, and she and Rob grabbed another beer and headed outside to sit on the patio. Zara sat down, and Rob took the seat across from her.

Rob pointed to the palm trees and thick foliage surrounding the patio. "It's really beautiful here. Much better than my patio that looks out over the apartment complex parking lot."

Zara smiled. "Yeah, and it's quiet. Peaceful."

Rob sipped his beer. "So what's next for Cause a Ripple?"

"You mean after the website is live?"

Rob nodded. "Yeah. Are you going to market the stones? What's your end game?"

Zara chewed on her lower lip, weighing how much she wanted to share. "I have a dream, if that's what you mean."

Rob sat up straighter. "What is it?"

Zara stretched her neck. "I know I'm a dreamer, but I want Cause a Ripple to inspire people and grow into a movement of goodness that spreads everywhere. I want people giving the stones to others who have made a difference. And I'd like to start a foundation. I'd like to donate a percentage of the sales profits to charity."

Rob's eyes widened. "Wow, that's a big dream."

Zara smiled. "Yeah, I know. But it's a dream worth having.

CHAPTER FOURTEEN

Jack listened as his cycle instructor, Dave, spoke. "Remember, always, always, always check your tire pressure and brakes. Make sure the axle is tight, and check the hook and loop fastener on the seat positioning strap and that your footrests work properly."

He walked over to Jack. "At the end of your pedal stroke, your arms should be slightly bent. Yours are fully extended, so let's fix that."

He adjusted Jack's cycle. "Also, check your helmet, safety flag, and mirror and make sure your cell phone is charged. Any questions?" He scanned the group, but no hands shot up. "Okay then, let's go!"

Jack winced. His breathing was labored. Ever since he started training with the local chapter of the Wounded Veterans Running Team, he'd been pushed beyond his limits. But he was getting stronger each day. So was Sam. Through Jack's encouragement, he'd joined too.

Sam finished his loop around the track and pulled up to Jack, who was catching his breath. "I can't believe I let you talk me into this." Sam sipped his energy drink. "And to think we gave up beer."

Jack laughed. "But we're much healthier, right? Besides, we were drinking too much beer." Jack patted his stomach. "No more beer gut."

Sam nodded.

Their trainer walked over to them. "You guys are doing great," Dave said. "Keep it up and you'll both be ready for the three-miler in a few months."

"The hand pedals hit my legs when I turn," Sam said.

"Coast through the turns with the hand pedals in the up position," Dave said. "And remember, changing gears will help save your arms and energy and help you ride longer distances."

Jack had to admit the running program was helping him rebuild his life. Unlike most of the guys, he had no family. It was one of the reasons he liked the military. Everyone looked out for each other, like family. And being a part of the team reminded him of being in the barracks with the guys. They'd joke, make fun of each other, and goof off. The camaraderie helped him as much as having a goal to go after.

When Dave set the handcycle in front of him for the first time, it was as if he'd opened a door. Jack never forgot how amazing riding it was. He felt free. Alive. And he had hope.

On the way back to their on-campus apartments, Jack and Sam decided to treat themselves to a beer—just one.

Sam lifted his bottle. "I'd forgotten just how much I enjoyed this stuff."

Jack laughed. "Don't get used to it."

"Can I ask you something?" Sam said.

Jack nodded.

"That stone you carry in your pocket. What's it for? I see you pull it out and rub it. Is it a good luck charm or something?"

Jack smiled. He carried the stone with him every day. He hadn't realized how often he reached for it until Sam brought it to his attention. "The nurse who took care of me when I first got here gave it to me." Jack ran his fingers through his hair. "First thing I did was whip it against the wall. It broke in two. Had to glue the pieces together. Never saw a heart-shaped stone until she gave it to me. And I was a jerk and broke it."

"I'm sure it's not the first heart a pretty boy like you has ever broken." Sam laughed.

"No, but it's the only heart that ever mattered."

Zara laid the cards, stones, and woven bags out on the kitchen table. Finally, she had all of the pieces. Stacey was coming over to help put the gift sets together. Zara had already done a couple. She punched a tiny hole in the thick business card and attached it to the bag by threading the string that closed the bag through the hole. She wanted the stone to be visible from the bag's opening, so she crumpled a piece of tan printer paper and stuffed it into the bag to elevate the stone.

It worked.

She heard Stacey's car pull into the driveway and went out to meet her. "So, what do you think?" She held up the tan bag.

Stacey smiled. "I love it! It's perfect." She followed Zara into the house. "Bobbi and Rob told me to say hi. He likes you, you know."

Zara sighed. "He asked me out when he came over to help me with the website. He's a sweetheart. He is. But he's just not the sweetheart for me. How's Tony?"

"I'm mad at him right now."

"Why?"

"He freakin' recorded me snoring."

Zara laughed. "What?"

They sat down at the table.

"The other night, he started snoring real loud. Man, it reminded me of my dad, which was so yuck. But anyhow, he's snoring and I couldn't fall asleep. I eventually drifted off, and when I woke up, he was looking right at me."

"I hate that."

"Me too. I asked him what was wrong, and he said I was snoring. To prove it, he pulled out his freakin' phone and played a video he'd recorded while I was asleep. That totally ticked me off. I told him the bedroom is a cell phone-free zone and made him delete the video."

"Did you tell him he snored?"

"Of course, but he didn't believe me. I should record him and see how he likes it."

They laughed.

Zara showed Stacey how to put the gift sets together. "I'll punch the holes in the cards, and you can attach them to the bags."

"How many should we do?" Stacey asked.

"Maybe twenty to start. I'm going to take a photo and upload it to my website. Then I'll make the site live."

"You've trademarked everything, right?"

Zara nodded. "Still trying to figure out how to set up a nonprofit foundation, but hopefully that will come in time."

Stacey threaded the string through the hole in the card. "What if they really take off and they start selling like mad?"

"That would be awesome. But I'd have to get help assembling them."

Stacey tied the string into a bow and set the bag down. "I did a story one time on sheltered workplaces. Businesses provide work to organizations that help mentally disabled people. Usually the focus is simple. Think copy centers or packing facilities. But it can involve simple product assembly where a few easy tasks are required. It might work for this."

"I never heard of that program before, but I love the idea of providing meaningful work that pays them."

"Me too," Stacey said. "Especially because it's tough for them to find jobs."

When they finished assembling the gift sets, they went into the living room to talk.

"Do you ever feel like the path you're on simply happened? Like you just sort of ended up on it?" Zara asked.

Stacey shook her head. "No, I definitely worked hard to get on the path I'm on. It was very deliberate. I've wanted to be a reporter since I was in junior high school. Is that how you're feeling? Like you just sort of ended up being a nurse?"

Zara picked up a throw pillow and wrapped her skinny arms around it. "Yes and no. I've always wanted to help people, to save people. But sometimes I wonder if I've been so busy running down the path that I haven't stopped to question whether I was going in the right direction."

"But you've stopped running now," Stacey said. "What have you decided? To continue on or change course?"

"I'm still trying to figure it out. But two things I've learned are that life is wildly unpredictable and achingly short. And if you have a dream, do it while you can."

That night after Zara crawled into bed, she picked up the pill puzzle. She kept it on her nightstand. She tilted the plastic puzzle, trying to get the little balls to go into the holes, but failed — again.

The next morning, the first thing Zara did was check her e-mail. She had a sale. Laura had bought six. She called Laura right away. "I love you, you know that?"

Laura laughed. "How did you know it was me?"

"Considering I see the customer's mailing address, it wasn't hard."

"But it's not my address."

"True, but it's the address of your school."

"It could be anyone who works at the school. My principal. The art teacher."

Zara smirked. "It could be, but it's not."

"Okay, you got me. I can't wait to get them. I love how they turned out. And the card with the ripples on it is perfect. I wish I could've helped you and Stacey put them together."

"You know," Zara said, "I would've given them to you at cost."

"I know, but I wanted to support you. It's not like I don't have the money to pay for six stones. One stone costs less than a glass of wine."

Zara sighed. "Thanks. I'll get them in the mail today. And, Laura, I love you. And I miss you."

"I miss you too."

Zara hung up the phone and poured a cup of coffee. She'd made a list of some local stores she planned to visit. Maybe they'd be willing to sell the stones for a commission. All she could do was ask them.

When she went for her morning run, she seemed to have more energy. The road blurred below her as she felt a surge of adrenaline. Her heart pounded to the beat of her racing feet. Sweat beaded on her forehead, and warmth seeped into her muscles. She pushed herself, running faster and harder, the air rushing in and out of her lungs. She was on autopilot when she saw her condo up ahead and sprinted to the finish. It was an exhilarating run.

She jumped into the shower, closed her eyes, and leaned into the spray of water. She felt alive and ready to tackle the day.

After mailing Laura's stones, Zara went to the cute little bookstore she'd found in town. She loved supporting independent bookstores—there were few left. She'd heard from a clerk during her last visit that the family-owned store had been in business for more than seventy years, despite the influx of big box bookstores and online retailers.

On her first visit, Zara had noticed an area near the front of the store that showcased items made by local artisans. She'd bought a colorful pair of earrings crafted from homemade glass beads. She hoped to pick up a matching bracelet while she was inquiring if the store would carry her stones.

When she walked in, she was surprised to see her neighbor, Lilli, behind the counter. "I didn't know you worked here."

Lilli tilted her head down, so her eyes peered over the top rim of her glasses. "Oh, hi, Zara. It's good to see you. I work just a couple of mornings a week. Gets me out of the house."

Zara smiled. "Well, this is a great place to work."

Lilli walked out from behind the counter. "Thanks. I'm glad I've run into you. I just learned my grandson is coming to visit next week. He's staying with us a couple of days before heading to Miami on business. I thought you might like to join us for dinner."

Zara's face felt hot, and she was sure she was turning as red as Lilli's lipstick. She had a feeling Lilli was trying to set her up. "Uh, sure. What night?"

"How about Tuesday?"

Zara nodded. "Tuesday's great."

Zara explained she wanted to talk to the owner about the possibility of carrying her stones. She gave Lilli the cliff notes and handed her one of the woven bags with the stone inside.

"What a lovely idea," Lilli said. "I have just the place to put these."

Zara followed Lilli over to a display table near the front door. Lilli moved some things around, making room for several of Zara's stones. "I'll keep the rest behind the counter and replenish them when these are sold."

Zara bit her lip, thankful for Lilli's help but worried she might get in trouble for not consulting her boss. "But shouldn't you ask the owner?"

Lilli patted her shoulder. "I'm the owner, dear. And I'd be glad to sell your stones. And because you're donating the proceeds to charity, I won't charge a commission."

Zara's jaw dropped, and her hand flew to her chest. "I'm sorry. I had no idea."

Lilli smiled. "The best things are often those we discover when we're not looking. Hopefully, my customers will discover your stones."

CHAPTER FIFTEEN

"You're a hard guy to track down," Tom told Jack when he found him in the apartment building lounge writing in his journal.

Jack looked up. "Didn't expect to see you here tonight. What's the special occasion?"

"I was in the area and hadn't seen you for a while. Thought I'd stop to see how things are going." Tom sat down across from Jack. "Still writing in your journal, I see."

Jack nodded.

"So how's the cycling?"

Jack closed his journal and laid his pen on top. "Great. It's a good workout. I'm going to get a cycle of my own. I'd always wanted a red sports car, so I'm going to get a red cycle."

Tom smiled. "Maybe I'll have to take a spin sometime."

"You should. You absolutely should. You might like it so much that you join the team."

"Whoa!" Tom held up his hands. "I wouldn't go that far. I barely have enough time to do the things I'm doing now."

Jack shifted in his seat. "How's school, anyway?"

"I have good days and bad days. Today was a bad day. My math professor surprised the class with a quiz."

"I always hated surprise quizzes in school," Jack said.

"Yeah, I wasn't prepared. Last night, Jen and I went to a birthing class, and I didn't have time to study. I'm pretty sure I bombed the quiz. But, hey, anyway. I didn't come here to talk about me."

"Don't let the bad days bring you down, Tom," Jack said. "Look at everything you've accomplished. The difference you've made in the lives of so many soldiers. The difference you'll make in the lives of kids when you get through school and become a guidance counselor."

Tom smiled. "Thanks. I should visit you more often. Is the journal writing helping?"

Jack patted the journal. "I've spilled a lot of anger onto these pages. Sometimes I go back and read entries and I'm shocked by the things I wrote. I was filled with so much hate. Kind of neat to see the progress I've made. I'm still angry, but I've definitely come a long way. I've even been looking into going to college."

Tom sat up straighter. "Really?"

"Yeah. Just been checking out stuff online. I've realized I'm the type of person who has to have goals. I have to have something to work toward. And when I accomplish one goal, I have to have another waiting. Pete, my PT, is great about pushing me to go farther, longer. Sometimes I get mad at him for pushing me so hard. But I'm glad he does. If he hadn't pushed me, I wouldn't be walking on prostheses and learning to ride a handcycle."

"My PT was like that too," Tom said. "Maybe it's in their DNA or something. Have any idea what you might like to study?"

"I like building things. I love anything with gears and gizmos. I'd love to build my own handcycle. Anyway, maybe mechanical engineering. I've always been pretty decent in math. My mom insisted I take the SAT my junior year in high school. I scored really high in the math area and not bad in the English. But after she died, I joined the military instead of going to college. It seemed like the sensible thing to do. I had no money, no family. The guys became my new family."

Tom nodded. "If you decide to apply to college and need a reference, you can count on me."

"Thanks," Jack said. "I'll let you know."

After leaving Lilli's bookstore, Zara visited an antique store Lilli had told her about and an art shop she stumbled upon along the way. Both owners agreed to sell her stones on consignment.

Zara thought a lot about what Lilli had said, repeating it over and over in her mind. *The best things are often those we discover when we're not looking.* She thought there was a lot of truth to that. Some of life's best moments were those she hadn't planned. They just sort of happened. Like going to church the night she heard the ripple sermon. Meeting Stacey in the self-help section of the bookstore. Taking care of Jack and being drawn to him in ways that scared her.

Over the next several days, Zara sold a few more stones. A Eucharistic minister she'd met at the pool showed a stone to some of the staff at his church, and they bought eighty to give to new parishioners. One of Lilli's customers, upon seeing the stone in her bookstore, ordered fifteen to give to her staff. She worked at a place that did repairs for assisted-living facilities. Lilli told Zara that Marge presented the stones to her staff during a lunch meeting and even had a pool of water for them to drop the stones into.

Zara felt good. It seemed like her dream was finally coming true. She knew she had to figure out how to market the stones, but what she really wanted to do first was set up the nonprofit foundation. From what Zara had learned, setting up the foundation was far more complicated and costly than she ever imagined it would be. So she clung onto the dream, still hoping that one day that too would become a reality.

Zara had just returned from mailing a stone at the post office and was about to make a dessert to take to Lilli's for dinner when her mom called.

"Hi, Mom."

"Oh, Dad. It's you. Why are you calling on Mom's phone?"

"Dad, I can barely hear you. You're breaking up."

His voice seemed caught in his throat as he tried to form the words. "It's your mother, Zara. I found her collapsed on the bathroom floor."

Zara's hand flew to her heart, and she cried as her dad described through broken speech what had happened.

"She was gardening when I left to play golf. When I returned, I found her sprawled on the bathroom floor. It looked like she was headed for the medicine cabinet. I think she got stung by bees. Just didn't make it in time to get her pills. Zara. I'm so sorry. I should have been there. I was golfing, for crying out loud. Golfing!"

By now, Zara was sobbing. She felt the heat of grief slide down her cheeks. The room was a blur, and she reached for tissues. "It's not your fault, Dad. I'll be home on the next available flight."

"Let me know your flight arrangements when you have them. I'll pick you up at the airport. We'll get through this—together."

After hanging up, she found a flight leaving in four hours and booked it. Then she called Lilli to tell her she wouldn't be coming to dinner, and she called Stacey to let her know what had happened.

"I'll take you to the airport," Stacey insisted.

"Don't worry. I can get a taxi."

"No. I'll be there in an hour to pick you up. No arguing. Do you need me to do anything?"

"No. You've done enough."

Next, she called Laura. As soon as Laura answered, Zara sobbed into the phone. Her throat tightened, and each word pitched higher than the last as she squeaked out the words. "Mom. Dad found her. Dead. On bathroom floor."

"Omigosh, Zara. I'm so sorry. I'll come home as soon as I can."

Zara's hands shook, and her breaths were short and shallow. She breathed in deeply, allowing the air to fill her lungs, and then exhaled. She tried to keep her voice from jumping octaves. "Thanks, but I know you have school. It's not like you can just up and leave your students."

"True, but I'll get a sub as soon as I can. I'll try to make it home in two days. Let me know what you need me to do."

Zara hung up, retrieved her suitcase from the closet, and stuffed it with clothes.

Stacey picked her up as she'd promised, and Zara cried the entire ride to the airport. "I should've been there for her. First Johnny, now Mom. My family's cursed."

Stacey pulled up to the passenger drop-off zone, parked, and climbed out of her car. She hugged Zara. "I wish I could go with you. I feel so bad you're flying home alone."

Zara sniffed. "Thanks, Stace. I'll be all right. Thanks for the ride and for being such a good friend and listening to me."

Stacey waved her finger. "Call me when you get in."

Zara nodded, turned, and rolled her bag toward the check-in line.

The next few days were a whirlwind of activity. Zara couldn't eat, and she couldn't sleep. Dark bags hung under her eyes. Her fingernails, which she managed to grow for the first time and had been painted red, were chewed down to the quick. When she and her dad picked out the casket, she thought she was going to pass out.

She sat in the funeral director's wood-paneled office, fanning herself with one of the sample programs he'd given her. "Is it hot in here?"

"No," her dad said. "I'm actually a little cold." He rubbed his left arm with his right.

"Do you want me to turn down the thermostat?" asked the director, a tall, thin man with ears too big for his skinny head that sported a patch of white fluff on top.

"No," Zara said. "I'll be fine. I think it's just my nerves."

"And here we have a nice cherry casket with a beige velvet liner." The funeral director pointed to the brochure spread out on the table. "Notice the gold molding around the base."

"What do you think, Zara?" her dad asked.

"It's okay."

"Just okay? I want it to be really nice. Your mother deserves something nice."

Zara mashed her lips together, trying to keep from crying. But she felt the tears coming on, like a migraine she couldn't stop, and knew she'd be dealing with them the rest of the day. "She's dead, Dad. What's it matter?"

Then Zara heaved, her sobs drenching everything around her. Her dad took her in his arms, and she collapsed and heaved against his shoulder. He kissed the top of her head. "It's okay, sweetie." He looked at the funeral director. "That one will be fine. And we'll use the program Zara picked out."

He walked Zara out to the car, drove her home, and helped her into bed. "Just rest, Zara."

Zara sniffed. "Sorry I'm such a mess, Dad."

He kissed her forehead. "You have nothing to be sorry about. Today was a tough day. It's going to be a tough several days, but we have to be strong for each other."

Zara nodded. "I love you, Dad."

"I love you more."

CHAPTER SIXTEEN

"What did you eat for breakfast this morning?" Sam asked Jack as he pulled his handcycle up beside his.

Jack guzzled his energy drink. "Just the normal. Two eggs, toast, and some bacon."

Sam wiped the sweat from his face with his towel. "If I'd eaten that this morning, I'd be upchucking it by now."

A double amputee whizzed by them on a handcycle.

"Man, he's fast," Sam said. "Think we'll ever be able to beat him?"

Jack licked his lips. "That's Charlie. He's good, and we can be just as good."

"Maybe you, but I'm not sure if I've got what that guy's got. That's some serious stuff."

"You know," Jack said, "Charlie's lucky to be alive. He was on a convoy in southern Afghanistan when a bomb went off and he caught fire. Almost died. The guy went through hell. A medically induced coma for a month, more than two years here recuperating, fighting his way back. Now look at him. Competing in marathons and studying to be a teacher."

"Damn," Sam said. "Thanks for making me feel like a jerk."

Jack laughed. "You're not a jerk, Sam. I'm learning that we don't always know what someone's gone through. Sometimes it's a lot worse than what you're dealing with. Guys like Charlie inspire me. He makes me want to push myself harder, go farther, faster."

"So you ever think about going back? What it would be like?"

"I did at first," Jack said. "I wanted to go back and kill as many enemies as I could. I figured I didn't have any family here, so why not? But then I met you, and Tom, and Pete, and everyone else. We're not fighting together in the desert, but we're fighting together here. To get better and to be as good as we can be."

"You talk a good game," Sam said.

"Well, it's easy when you believe what you're saying."

"Maybe you ought to try preaching. You'd look good in a white robe."

Jack laughed. "Then I'd have to listen to your confessions. I'm not sure I'd be able to handle that. Want to go one more time around?"

Sam took off, pedaling his handcycle harder and faster than he ever had. It took all Jack had to catch up to him. Then they raced to the finish line together.

"I think we're ready for the big race," Jack said.

Sam nodded. "We're as ready as we'll ever be."

Zara stared into the bathroom mirror. She looked tired. Her eyelids drooped, and she couldn't stop yawning. She didn't want to wear a lot of makeup because she figured she'd be crying, but she applied a little bit of eye shadow and some waterproof mascara. And she did her best to cover up the gray bags that hung heavy under her eyes.

She decided to wear a simple black dress with three-quarter sleeves and a round neck. She added a belt.

When she walked downstairs, she found her dad in the living room looking through one of the photo albums her mom kept on the bookshelf next to the fireplace.

He looked up. "You look beautiful, Zara. Just like your mother."

Zara walked over and hugged her dad. She sat down beside him, and they looked at the album together.

Zara pointed to a photo of her and Johnny standing beside Mickey and Minnie Mouse at Walt Disney World. "I remember that trip. We were so excited. Mom bought us autograph books, and we spent hours chasing the characters for autographs."

Her dad smiled. "Yeah, we had some good times, didn't we?"

"We had the best, Dad." She hugged him again. "Do you think if we had known Mom and Johnny would die so young, we would've lived our lives differently?"

Her dad didn't reply right away. "The thing about life, Zara, is that you should live it without regrets. Would-haves. Should-haves. Could-haves. They're a waste. Live in the moment. Cherish the moment because we never know when it will end. A bomb goes off. Bees sting. We don't get do-overs. When bad things happen, we need to pick ourselves off the ground and keep going. It's not easy. Tonight won't be easy. But we'll get through it together."

"But you seem to be so calm about everything. Not that you're not grieving, but you're handling it so much better than me."

"Oh, sweetie. Believe me, I have my moments. I'll roll over in bed expecting your mother to be there. Or I'll walk into the office expecting to see her working on her laptop. I might project calmness, but I'm just as torn up inside as you. We've been through a lot, and it seems so unfair."

He closed the album and returned it to the bookshelf. By the time he and Zara had arrived at the church, the cherry casket with the gold molding around the middle was placed in front, flanked by rows of vases and baskets filled with just about every kind of flower.

A line of people snaked through the sanctuary and out the front door. Zara was surprised by how many people came to pay their respects. It wasn't that long ago she stood in this same spot with both her parents, receiving visitors who came to say good-bye to Johnny. Her mom would be buried beside him in the family plot her parents had purchased long ago. Johnny would have a sledding partner.

Zara listened as visitors shared stories about her mom. Some of them were childhood friends. Others knew her from the childcare center she owned.

A woman who looked to be in her mid-fifties limped toward the casket. She said a prayer before making the sign of the cross on her chest. She turned to Zara and her dad. "Mrs. Peede was the nicest woman I've ever met." She dabbed her teary eyes with a tissue. "She helped me when I fell on some hard times. Couldn't afford daycare. She took my son in and told me to pay whatever I could. If it wouldn't have been for her, I don't know what I would've done. Your mom was one heck of a lady. I'll never forget what she did for us. Jerome just turned thirty. He asked me to express his condolences as well."

Zara and the woman hugged. "Thanks for sharing your story."

"So your son's doing well, then?" her dad asked.

"Oh, my, yes." The woman's bright smile took up most of her face. "Matter a fact, he just became a daddy. Sweet little girl. Named her Rose, after me."

Zara's mother, who had a degree in early childhood education, started the center before Zara and Johnny were born. Over the years, it grew and had become one of the most respected daycare centers in the area. Zara helped out at the center throughout school and then over college breaks. She loved the children and was proud of what her mom had built. Her mom had an incredible staff, which took care of children from birth through kindergarten. It had grown so much over the years that she built an addition to add six classrooms. Zara knew she and her dad would have to discuss what to do with the center, and she hoped he'd like her idea.

A high school friend of Johnny's stepped forward and hugged Zara. "I'm so sorry, Zara. Wish I was seeing you again under better circumstances."

"Thanks, Matt."

"I'll never forget the time your mom gave me money for our senior class trip. Guess Johnny told her I wasn't going to go because my parents couldn't afford it." He rubbed his neck. "Next thing I knew, I was called down to the office and the guidance counselor told me my trip had been paid in full. Then he hands me an envelope with a hundred dollar bill in it and said, 'I was told to give you this for spending.' I'd never seen a hundred dollar bill before."

Zara felt like she had a rock stuck in her throat but managed to ask, "How did you know it was my mom?"

"I didn't. Not at first. I suspected it, of course. But Johnny let it slip when we were in line for a ride. He hadn't realized he'd told me. And I didn't say anything. Figured I should keep it to myself. Never told anyone that story until now."

Zara cried as Matt wrapped his thick arms around her. "Thank you for telling me that story," Zara said. "I'm glad you shared it with me."

Matt nodded. "I thought you should know the difference your mom made in my life."

One by one, Zara greeted those who came to pay their respects. They all had stories, and Zara was stunned that so many of them involved her mom doing something nice for the person. A bill that was paid. A helping hand when it was needed. Her heart was warmed by the difference her mom had made in so many lives. Zara wished her mom had known how far reaching the ripples she'd created had gone.

After everyone had left, Zara walked over to her mom's casket. She kissed her mom on the cheek then tucked a Cause a Ripple stone in her folded hands, along with a red rose.

"I love you, Mom. I'll see you on the other side."

CHAPTER SEVENTEEN

Jack inhaled deeply. It was his first race.

He couldn't believe after months of practice, he was at the starting line. All the runners, able bodied and disabled, were lined up in their corrals, their racing bibs attached to their shirts. Sam was beside him along with a slew of other riders. They had trained for this race for months, and the day had finally arrived.

So many emotions swirled through his head. Thanks to a generous donor, he had a custom-made red handcycle that was the perfect fit. He touched his pants pocket, making sure his good-luck charm was there. He took the stone Zara had given him everywhere. He even slept with it under his pillow.

"Remember," Coach Dave told the team. "Your cycle doesn't run you—you run your cycle. Do the best you can and have fun."

Jack had a competitive streak, but when it came to handcycling, he didn't compete against others—he competed against himself. He pushed himself to go faster, farther. To beat his individual times, not the times of others.

The cycle had given him life and a sense of confidence. Maybe he could encourage others like him. If he could show them what they could achieve, maybe they'd try. Jack realized a disabled vet's biggest hurdle was believing his life wasn't over. Until he'd met

Tom, that's what he'd thought. But he learned that losing his legs wasn't the end, but rather, a new beginning.

Adapt and overcome, Coach Dave always said.

Jack licked his lips, waiting for the signal. The horn pierced the air, and the cycles broke out. A sea of moving color. Red, yellow, blue, and green.

The five-mile course through New York's Central Park was hilly, and Jack had to downshift quite a bit. But it was invigorating. People lined the route, along the southern edge of the park, north on East Drive, up Cat Hill, along West Drive, gathering by the hundreds at the Transverse near West Sixty-Ninth Street.

As Jack crossed the finish line, he was greeted by thunderous cheers and applause. A reporter approached him. "Congratulations."

Jack sucked in a mouthful of air and quickly released it. "Thanks."

"I understand this was your first race. How's it feel?"

Jack wiped the sweat off his face. "Incredible."

"Is there anything you'd like to tell other wounded veterans who might want to try handcycling?"

"Yes," Jack said. "Anybody can do it. You just have to have the willpower."

Sam pulled up next to Jack, and they high-fived each other. "We did it, bro."

They watched as others crossed the finish line. A girl running with a prosthetic leg, her chestnut brown pigtails flopping like fish out of water. An older boy in a wheelchair, flanked by his parents. A guy running with two prosthetic legs. Jack and Sam cheered for them all.

Jack pointed to the man who looked to be about his age. "That's going to be us next year," he told Sam.

"He's amazing, isn't he?" Sam said.

Jack nodded. "I ran into him in the hotel lobby. He told me this was his first year racing on his two prosthetic legs. He'd always cycled but wanted to run it."

"So what's his story?" asked Sam.

"Same as ours. Roadside bomb. Humvee he was in hit a tripwire."

"Thanks," Sam said.

"For what?"

"For pushing me to cycle. It's the best thing that's happened since getting injured."

Zara sat behind the podium, waiting to be introduced. Her curly hair tumbled over her narrow shoulders. She wore a black dress with a necklace she'd made using a Cause a Ripple stone. Her hands were sweaty. She wasn't used to speaking in public, but she couldn't turn down the invitation.

The company hosting the banquet manufactured handcycles used by veterans. It also sponsored all twenty-five participants in the Central Park race, paying for their travel expenses, racing fees, and lodging. The banquet culminated the event.

Zara learned about the company and its race sponsorship through Lilli's grandson, who was the company's attorney. When she contacted the company and pitched her idea of giving stones to the participants, the executives invited her to present them at the banquet. Because of a prior commitment, she hadn't been able to attend the race. In fact, her plane had just landed a couple hours ago. The company had a limo waiting for her at the airport, and she'd hurried to get ready in time.

She looked out over the crowded room that was packed with veterans and their families.

Jack walked into the dining room and found his assigned table. He sat with Sam, and another racer, and the racer's wife. He picked up the program next to his dinner plate. He opened it and read, *Presentation of Stones by Zara Peede.*

Jack's heart started to race. Instinctively, he felt for the stone in his pocket. It was there. He looked around and spotted her sitting on the stage. He swallowed hard. She looked more beautiful than he'd remembered. Would she recognize him?

A voice boomed from the microphone. Jack barely listened as the company president went on and on about how proud he was of the veterans— what they had accomplished and what great role models they were. Then he heard Zara's name, and he sat up straighter.

"We are honored to have with us today Zara Peede. Zara is the founder of Cause a Ripple, which recognizes those who have made a difference or, as Zara says, caused positive ripples through their actions. I'll let Zara explain the organization and say a few words. Then we'd like to present each of you with a stone. When your name is called, please come forward. Zara will come down off the stage to greet you as I read the names. But first, a few words from Zara."

Zara stood at the podium, her note cards in her sweaty hands. She inhaled deeply and exhaled, trying to calm her nerves. She turned to the man and nodded. "Thank you for inviting me to join you today."

She looked out over the room and smiled. "And thank you, race participants, for causing so many ripples. You've inspired so many people. Your determination, will power, and commitment are simply amazing. Please give yourselves a round of applause."

The room filled with clapping and a few shrill whistles. Zara waited until the noise died down before continuing. "I was a nurse at Walter Reed."

At the mention of Walter Reed, the room once again erupted into thunderous applause. This time it was louder and lasted longer.

Zara waited for the room to quiet. "As I was saying, I was a nurse at Walter Reed before starting Cause a Ripple." She went on to describe Cause a Ripple, its purpose, and how it came to be. As she told them about the sermon, tears gathered in the corner of her eyes.

"I wasn't a church-going person, but that day, that sermon changed my life. I felt as though the pastor was speaking to me. I'd never realized just how much we impact others. From that day on, my life changed. It started to happen gradually. I began to see the good in other people. A child who held open a door for an elderly man. A teacher who stayed after school to help a struggling student. A man who rebuilt bicycles and donated them to the poor. And I began to praise them and tell them why. Odd, the more good things you notice and praise, the more ripples you help create. Pointing out the positive encouraged them to do even more wonderful things."

Zara took a deep breath. "And that's why I'm here today. All of you have created ripples. You've impacted thousands of people by what you've done. Not only by serving in the military but by also participating in today's race. What an incredible accomplishment! I know how hard your journey has been. I cared for wounded soldiers after they arrived from Germany. I know the passion and commitment it takes to conquer your fears, and overcome your doubts, and realize that life isn't over—it's just a new beginning. Attitude is everything, and each of you has shown what a difference the right attitude can make.

"Think of the thousands of people who lined that race route today, the wounded vets in beds at Walter Reed. You've inspired them all. And in appreciation for being positive role models, I'd like to give each of you a stone. It's a simple reminder of the ripples you've created. Good luck as you continue your journey, and thank you for showing others what they can accomplish if they only believe."

Zara looked back at the company president, and he stood, joining her at the podium. "Thank you, Zara, for sharing your story and for being here today. Can we have a round of applause for this incredible lady?"

Once again, the room erupted in applause. Then one Marine near the front stood, and soon everyone in the room who could was standing and clapping.

Zara's hand flew to her heart. "Thank you. Thank you so much."

The company president nodded, and when the applause died down, he spoke. "As I call your name, please come forward to accept your stone."

Zara stepped off the stage and walked to the side where a small table held twenty-five stone gift sets. The president began announcing the names of each recipient.

"Nathan John Bowers."

Zara watched as a man with one prosthetic leg walked toward her. She picked up a stone gift set, handed it to him, and shook his hand.

"David James Nade."

"Tyler Morgan Gross."

Each time, a soldier approached Zara, walking on prosthetic limbs. Some were missing one leg, but most were missing both.

"Samuel Lee Matthews."

Sam pushed back his chair, and Jack smiled. He watched Sam walk toward Zara. Sam was the only one in the group who had a prosthetic arm.

It looked like Jack was the last one. He pushed out his chair, waiting for his name to be called.

"Jack Thomas Quinlan."

Zara mashed her lips together. She felt as if there was a boulder stuck in her throat. She hadn't seen the list of race participants. She had no idea Jack was one of the recipients.

Her heart pounded as she watched Jack walk toward her. She couldn't believe how tall he was. He still had his curls, but his hair was shorter. And he was clean shaven, something he rarely was when she'd been his nurse. The last time she'd seen him, he was lying in bed, anger spewing from him like hot lava.

A million thoughts flooded her. She remembered the stone she'd given him and how he'd whipped it against the wall. She could hear his voice. *Listen, Nurse Buttinsky. If it's not a magic stone and can't bring back my legs, what good is it?*

She was about to give him another stone. How would he react? Was he still so angry? Even though she was scared of his reaction, she had butterflies in her stomach. He was the only guy who made her feel like that. Even now. After all this time.

When he was a foot away from her, he stopped. She watched as he reached into his pocket and pulled out something. He held out his fist and turned it over so his bended fingers were on top. He opened his fingers to reveal the heart-shaped stone in the palm of his hand. He smiled. "I'll take the new stone, but this one will always be special."

Zara's hand flew to her heart. She inhaled deeply, slowly, and exhaled quickly. She handed him the gift set. "You look great, Jack. I'm proud of you."

Jack nodded and turned toward his table. Zara watched as he walked to his seat. She wanted to run after him and hug him, but she didn't. She felt like her feet were glued to the floor and suddenly became aware that everyone was watching her watching Jack. It was an awkward moment, and Zara suddenly felt that she should offer some sort of explanation. She returned to the podium.

"Ladies and gentleman. Jack Quinlan was one of my patients. I cared for him when he returned from Afghanistan. The last time I saw him, he was lying in a bed. I had no idea he was among the honorees today. Congratulations, Jack, and congratulations to all of you."

The sound of chairs scraping the tile floor filled the room. Everyone was standing and clapping.

"Thank you, Zara," the company president said. "You've certainly caused ripples today."

CHAPTER EIGHTEEN

Sam nudged Jack's shoulder. "That's her. The chick you've been pining after all these months."

Jack nodded.

"And that stone you carry everywhere—she's the one who gave it to you, isn't she?"

Again, Jack nodded. "Zara gave me the stone before she left the medical center."

Sam shook his head. "You're one lucky guy."

"What do you mean?"

"Everyone in this room felt the heat between you two."

Jack cleared his throat. "I have no idea what you're talking about."

"I'm talking about you and her. Hot, man. Watching you two was like watching two magnets trying to keep apart. Go for it, bro."

Jack ran his fingers through his hair. "I was thinking about hanging out here a bit afterward. Do you mind?"

"Heck no. Tyler asked me if I wanted to go out with him and Dave. Well, they invited both of us. I was supposed to ask you. But I'll go with them, and you and the lady can talk."

After dessert, Jack stayed at the table, watching as the room emptied. He felt a hand on his shoulder and looked up. "You look great, Jack," Zara said.

He smiled. "You too."

Zara shifted the manila envelope she was holding in her right hand to her left. "I'd love to catch up. That is, if you have time."

"I'd like that." Jack pushed out his chair and stood.

Zara looked up at him. "I had no idea you were so tall."

Jack scratched his head. "I hope that's not a bad thing."

"Oh, not at all. I'm, um, just not used to it."

Jack grinned and led Zara to the hotel bar, where they found a quiet table in the corner. Zara ordered a glass of chardonnay, and Jack ordered whiskey and coke.

Jack's dark eyes pierced Zara's. "I never thought I'd see you again."

Tears formed in the corners of Zara's eyes. "I had no idea you were one of the honorees. What an accomplishment, Jack."

Jack sighed. "Guess I look a lot different than the last time you saw me."

Zara nodded. "You look amazing. And you're walking and racing."

"I'm starting to run too," Jack said. "I want to run this race next year on prosthetic legs."

Zara smiled. "I'm glad you realized your life wasn't over."

"I'm not going to lie. It took a while. But your stone helped. I kept it with me always. It was a reminder of what you wrote in your letter."

"Which part?"

Jack cleared his throat and swallowed hard as if he was preparing to deliver an important speech. "'The only way a dream can die is if you let it.'"

Zara smiled. "And you didn't let it die, Jack. I'm so happy for you. And proud. Really proud."

[125]

Jacked pulled the stone out of his pocket and held it in the palm of his hand. "That's why this one is extra special."

Zara touched the stone. "It seems like I gave you this stone a lifetime ago."

Jack looked into her eyes. "I know what you mean. I've come a long way since the day I whipped it against the wall and broke it."

"But you put it back together just like you've put your life back together."

"Yeah, but I wish I wouldn't have broken the stone in the first place. I ruined something that was perfect."

Zara leaned into the table and stared into Jack's eyes. "I've learned that nothing in life is perfect, Jack. We think it is. We desperately want it to be. But there's beauty in imperfection. The flaws mean something. They count for something. They matter."

Jack wrapped his fingers around the stone and made a tight fist. "'There's beauty in imperfection.' I like that. I'll remember that." He put the stone back in his pants pocket.

The waitress approached the table with their drinks, one in each hand. "Here we go. Is there anything else I can get you?"

Jack looked at Zara, and she shook her head. "I think we're good for now."

After the waitress walked away, Jack lifted his glass. "A toast."

Zara lifted her glass.

"To Zara, the Stone Giver."

Zara laughed. "Stone Giver?"

Jack shrugged. "It fits!"

"And to Jack," Zara said. "Who inspired so many people today and has given so much to the world."

Their glasses touched, and they sipped their drinks.

"So, tell me about the stones. About Cause a Ripple."

Jack listened as a narrative of the last six months unfurled over the next hour. Zara's move to Florida. Launching Cause a Ripple. Creating the website. Finding a company to manufacture the stones.

Figuring out how to package the product and market it. And establishing the Cause a Ripple Foundation.

"Wow," Jack said. "You've been one busy lady. And are you working? I mean, this sounds like a full-time job."

Zara sipped her wine. "Actually, I have a full-time job."

"Ah, so you returned to nursing."

"Well, not exactly. Although if there's a skinned knee, I'm there to take care of it."

Jack's brows furrowed. "You lost me."

"My mom died," Zara explained.

Jack shifted in his seat. "I'm sorry. I had no idea."

"Thank you. I was a complete basket case after Johnny died."

"You mean your mom."

"No. Johnny, my brother."

"He died too?" Jack asked.

Zara nodded. "I guess I never told you about Johnny. He was a bomb disposal expert, and he was killed by an IED while on foot patrol."

Jack reached across the table and touched Zara's arm. "Why didn't you tell me? I had no idea what you were going through."

"It's not something a nurse tells a wounded vet who's just returned from Hell."

Jack rubbed his neck. "Man, oh, man. I wish I'd known."

Zara sighed. "It was one of the reasons I left Walter Reed. Caring for the wounded was a daily reminder that I couldn't care for my brother. I couldn't fix him. Everywhere I looked, I saw Johnny, and I needed a break. I wasn't sleeping, and I was starting to become best friends with my bottle of sleeping pills."

"I can definitely relate to the not sleeping," Jack said.

"Anyway, my mom owned a daycare center. She started it when she was my age, after she and Dad married, and years before she had kids of her own. She graduated college with a degree in early-childhood education, and the daycare was her dream. Over the years, it grew. Mom moved to a bigger building, added classrooms and staff. It's become perhaps the most respected daycare center in the area. After she died, I decided to take it over."

"That's a lot of responsibility," Jack said.

Zara nodded. "But I love it. I love being able to make a difference in children's lives. I try to see qualities in children that most others overlook. So I try to praise them and explain why I'm doing it. Maybe they were polite, or shared their toy, or helped the teacher. Or maybe they tried hard."

"So you're causing ripples among the very young."

"Sort of, I guess."

Jack sipped his whiskey. "That's a long way from nursing."

"True, but I'm still caring for people, just little people."

The waitress stopped by their table. "Can I get you anything else?"

"Water," Jack said.

Zara nodded. "Make that two." She turned to Jack. "So tell me about your life."

Jack ran his fingers through his hair. "There's not much to tell. I've been writing in the journal you gave me."

"Great," Zara said. "Has it helped?"

"Yeah. And getting involved in handcycling has really helped. Coach Dave is tough. Almost as tough as Pete."

"How's Pete, anyway?"

"As demanding as ever."

Zara waved her hand. "But look at you. If it wasn't for Pete…"

"I know, I know." Jack sighed. "I owe the guy a lot. And you too."

Zara blushed. "I wasn't there that long. I left you."

"Yeah, and I wasn't happy when Nurse Donna walked into my room instead of you. But I didn't know about Johnny and your reasons for leaving. I read your letter every day. You said in your letter that one day we might meet again. Well, here we are."

Zara smiled and lifted her glass. "Yes, here we are." She sipped her wine, savoring the flavor before letting the liquid slip down her throat. "So how long are you in New York?"

"Tomorrow yet. I've never been to New York and decided to do some sightseeing. How about you?"

"Same. I haven't been to New York for a few years, so I figured I'd take in some sights. See what's new."

"You up for company?" Jack asked. "I'd love to have someone show me around. On second thought, I'd probably just slow you down."

"Nonsense." Zara waved. "I'd love to show you around. Are you staying here?"

Jack nodded.

"How about we meet for breakfast tomorrow morning in the hotel dining room?"

"That sounds great," Jack said. "What time?"

"Eight thirty. Or is that too early?"

"No, it's perfect."

Zara yawned.

"Looks like someone's ready for bed."

"It's been a long day." Zara explained she'd only arrived a couple hours before the banquet.

"I'll walk you to your room."

"You don't have to," Zara said.

"I insist."

Jack stood and pulled out Zara's chair. They walked to the elevator and stepped inside. "What floor?" Jack asked.

"Four."

Jack pressed the button. When the elevator door opened, he followed Zara out into the hallway. Zara stopped when they reached her door. She turned to look at Jack. "Thank you for walking me back. I really enjoyed catching up."

Jack smiled. "Me too."

Zara slid her key card into the slot and stepped inside, waving bye one last time before she closed the door. She placed her hand over her thumping heart and sat on the edge of her bed. She thought Jack was absolutely stunning in his dark suit, white shirt, and red tie. It was hard to believe he was the same guy she'd held in her arms trying to calm after a nightmare.

Zara yawned again and undressed. She jumped into the shower and let the hot water massage her back. By the time she finished, her body felt relaxed, and she fell into bed. But first, she called the front desk for a wake-up call. She didn't want to miss breakfast with Jack.

CHAPTER NINETEEN

Zara searched her suitcase, trying to find something flattering to wear. She wished she'd packed her sundress. It'd be cooler than the jeans she brought. At least she packed her sneakers. The new four-inch stilettos she'd worn the night before crushed her toes and left her feet hurting. As much as she loved wearing heels, the pain in the ball of her foot seemed to get worse over time.

She wondered where to take Jack. Was he a museum type of person or a Broadway show kind of guy? Maybe he was both. Zara leaned in toward the bathroom mirror and brushed her eyelashes with mascara. She wasn't one for heavy makeup. She preferred the natural look. A touch of lip gloss and she was ready to meet Jack.

He was waiting for her at the entrance to the dining room. He looked handsome in his khaki shorts and baby blue polo shirt. His curly hair was still damp, and Zara detected a woodsy scent.

Zara smiled. "Good morning. I hope you weren't waiting long."

"Just arrived." Jack opened the door for her.

The maître d led them to a table tucked in the corner. As they passed tables, Jack couldn't help but notice the attention he was attracting from diners. Their eyes shifted to his legs, which resembled metal rods, and then quickly away. Jack was getting used to the stares and whispers, but the attention still bothered him. He felt like General Grievous with his droid-like legs sticking out of his shorts.

The maître d handed them menus, explaining the breakfast buffet. "You may order off the menu if you wish." He bowed slightly before leaving.

Jack opened the menu. "I'm not used to eating in such fancy places."

"Well, I hope you enjoy it." Zara scanned the menu. "I was thinking about getting the buffet, but I'm reconsidering. I always overeat when I go to a buffet."

Jack looked up from the menu. "You certainly don't look it."

Zara smiled. "Thanks. What about you. Buffet?"

"Actually, no. I think I'll get the Spanish omelet with home fries."

The waitress, who was curvy and a little thick in the hips, came to the table holding a carafe of coffee. "Would either of you like coffee?"

Zara turned up her cup. "Yes, please. With cream."

"And you?" She looked at Jack.

Jack turned over his cup. "Black for me."

The waitress filled their mugs. "I'll be right back to take your order."

Jack blinked. "Wow! She looks a lot like my mom except for the red hair. Mom had brown."

Zara poured cream into her coffee. "Does that bother you?"

Jack shrugged. "I miss her at times. Especially when this happened. I had no one—except you." He stared at Zara, and just when she was about to say something, the waitress returned. Zara waited for her to pull out a pad to write down their order but then realized she wasn't using one.

"I'll have the French toast with a side of bacon," Zara said.

"And I'll take the Spanish omelet with home fries."

The waitress nodded and left.

"I'd never be able to remember the orders unless I wrote them down," Zara said. "I admire waitresses and waiters who can do that. So, back to your mom. You never told me what happened to her. If you ever want to talk about it…" Zara's voice drifted off.

Jack sipped his coffee. "There's really nothing to talk about. I came home one night and found her dead. I learned later she'd been ill for a while. I think she was trying to hold on until I graduated from high school. She wrote a letter, though. I found it in her dresser. I had to clean out all her stuff."

Zara shook her head. "Oh, Jack. I'm so sorry. That must've been awful. Did you have any help?"

"A couple of my buddies came over, but they were busy with their own lives. I certainly didn't expect them to drop everything to help me. I was supposed to go to college. Mom had saved some money over the years, and I got some academic scholarships. But after she died, I figured what was the point? So I joined the Marines instead. But I kind of wish I would've went to college—especially now." He patted his thighs.

Zara listened, afraid to move because she didn't want to startle Jack and make him self-conscious about what he was sharing. "You can still go to school, you know?"

Jack nodded. "I've been thinking about that. Tom, my peer supporter, is studying to become a school guidance counselor. He wants to work with kids."

The waitress had left the carafe of coffee, and Zara topped off her mug. "What would you like to do?"

Jack sighed. "I like to build things. I was going to go to school for mechanical engineering. Not sure I'd be able to do it now."

"Why not?" Zara asked.

Jack shrugged. "Maybe I'm not smart enough anymore."

Zara laughed. "You're probably smarter, and you can always take courses or get tutored on the subjects you might be rusty on."

Jack rolled his eyes. "Like math."

Zara smiled. "Like math."

The waitress returned and slid the Spanish omelet in front of Jack and the French toast in front of Zara.

"It looks delicious," Zara said.

"Can I get you anything else?" the waitress asked.

Jack looked at Zara, who shook her head. "I think we're good for now. Thanks."

Jack sprinkled salt over his omelet. "I don't think you told me how your mom died. Was she ill?"

Zara poured syrup over her French toast. "No. It was quite sudden. Very unexpected. And freaky."

Jack furrowed his brows. "Freaky?"

Zara explained how her mom was deathly allergic to bees and how she'd been stung while gardening.

"She went inside to get pills but never made it. Dad found her collapsed on the bathroom floor."

Jack watched as Zara's eyes turned glassy. "I'm so sorry, Zara. That's awful."

Zara nodded. "At least she's with Johnny now." She cut her French toast into tiny pieces. "Would you like to try it?"

Jack held up his hand. "No, I have plenty."

"The omelet looks yummy."

"It is. Want a piece?"

Zara shook her head. "So what would you like to do today? Go to a museum? See a show? Visit the Empire State building?"

"I'm up for anything, although I'd really like to see the 9/11 memorial."

"We'll go there first," Zara said. "And see how you feel after that. You might want to come back to the hotel and rest in the afternoon. We could do the Empire State building in the evening."

Jack squeezed ketchup over his home fries. "Sounds like a plan."

They finished eating, and the waitress returned to ask if they wanted anything else.

Zara glanced at her plate. It looked as if she had hardly touched her French toast. "It was delicious, but I can't even finish what I ordered."

"I'm done too," Jack said.

The waitress returned and placed the check face down in front of Jack. He flipped it over and blinked.

Zara jerked toward Jack. "What's wrong?"

He handed the check to Zara. On the check was written: *Thank you for serving.*

Zara scanned the restaurant trying to figure out who'd paid their bill, but everyone seemed knee-deep in conversation. "What a nice gesture."

Jack sniffed. "Yeah. Very nice. But how did they know?"

"They probably put two and two together," Zara said. "The race was all over the news and..."

Jack nodded. "And my legs. They give me away every time."

Zara smiled. "Well, they are really sexy."

Jack chuckled. "Thanks. I work hard to keep them that way."

"Seriously, Jack. You're doing really well with your new legs. And I can see your upper body has become very strong."

Jack flexed his right arm. "Just like Popeye."

They laughed and finished their coffee. Jack laid a twenty on the table. "Are you ready?"

Zara gathered her purse and stood. "We can ask the maître d to get us a taxi."

Jack followed Zara through the restaurant to the podium where the maître d stood. Again, he could feel the stares of diners. When the cab arrived, they crawled in.

"Take us to the 9/11 Memorial," Zara said.

The middle-aged driver nodded and weaved in and out of traffic, pulling up to the site of the former World Trade Center complex. Jack and Zara stepped out and walked across the Memorial plaza, shaded by hundreds of swamp white oak trees. Neither of them spoke as they came upon the recessed reflecting pools set within the footprints of the Twin Towers. The sights and sounds of the bustling metropolis faded.

As they stood next to the bronze parapets surrounding the North Pool, Jack trembled. The parapets contained the names of those who had died. There were so many of them. As they watched the water flow away into the abyss, Zara burst into tears. Instinctively, Jack put his arm around her, and she buried her face into his chest, sobbing.

Jack whispered. "It's okay. I'm here. Everything's going to be okay."

For a few seconds, Jack had forgotten he was standing on prosthetic legs. The only thing that mattered to him was Zara. Odd, he thought, that I'm comforting her. It had always been the other way around.

Jack led her to a stone bench, and they sat. Children played nearby. Their laughter, a reminder of life and hope, seemed out of place in that moment.

Zara sniffed. "Sorry I'm such a mess. It's just that 9/11 changed everything. Johnny came home from school that night and declared he was going into the Marines. I remember it like it was this morning. It was a gorgeous day. The sky a beautiful blue. We had spaghetti for dinner that night. Mom started the conversation. She wanted to know what the teachers had told us and if we had any questions. That's when Johnny said he was going to kill the bad guys. From that day on, the Marines were all he talked about. Maybe if 9/11 hadn't happened, Johnny would still be here."

Jack brushed Zara's blonde curls off her face so he could look into her green eyes. "And maybe he wouldn't be. Life doesn't always go the way we want it to."

Zara sniffed. "I'm such an insensitive jerk. I should be comforting you."

Jack smiled. "It's nice to be the one to give the comfort. Especially to someone I care about."

Zara bit her lower lip and looked down at the ground to avoid Jack's eyes.

Jack touched her back. "Sorry if I made you feel uncomfortable."

Zara straightened and turned to him. "You didn't. It's just that, well, I was your nurse."

"*Was* is the operative word," Jack said. "You stopped being my nurse a long time ago."

"I know," Zara said. "But still."

Jack shifted in his seat. "Still what?"

"Still, we shouldn't get too close."

Jack shook his head. "No! That's not fair. We both know there's more to our relationship than you being my nurse. I felt it the first time you walked into my room, and I know you felt it too. There's something between us. Something special." Jack put his hands on either side of Zara's head and stared into her eyes. "I care about you, Zara. I have since the moment I laid my eyes on you. We both know that life is short. We never know what's going to happen. But I will not let you slip away again without fighting for you."

Zara eyes widened as she listened. Her heart raced. She hadn't expected him to give such an emotional speech. A renegade tear slid down his cheek.

An old man standing nearby had stopped to listen when Jack raised his voice. "Shut up and kiss her," the man barked.

Jack and Zara looked at him. He was dressed in dark pants and a shirt that looked like they hadn't been washed in weeks. "Go on. Kiss her." He winked. "Stop wasting time, boy."

Jack and Zara turned toward each other. Zara shrugged. Jack lifted her chin, and their lips touched.

They heard the old man chuckle, but when they looked back, he was gone.

CHAPTER TWENTY

Zara opened her hotel room door and collapsed onto the bed. After visiting the 9/11 memorial and museum, she and Jack had decided to return to the hotel to rest. They planned to meet later for dinner and visit the Empire State Building.

Zara picked up her cell phone and called Laura, speaking before Laura had time to answer. "We kissed. And it was electric."

"Whoa. Back up. Who kissed?"

Zara stacked two bed pillows to lay her head on. "Sorry. Jack and me."

"Jack as in Jack, your former patient?"

"Yes." Zara lay back on the pillows, and her head sank into the softness.

"You went to the medical center?"

"No, no, no. In New York. Today. At the 9/11 Memorial."

"Maybe you ought to start at the beginning," Laura said. "You lost me at kiss and electric."

Zara explained she'd caught up with Jack at the banquet for the wounded veterans participating in the Central Park Race.

"So you had no idea he was a participant until they read his name?" Laura asked.

"Correct. And we talked afterward and decided to spend the day together."

"So where's he now?"

"Resting. We're both resting."

"Together?"

"No, not together. He's in his room, and I'm in mine. We're going to have dinner later and tour the Empire State Building."

"Sounds romantic."

"That's what I'm afraid of. We can't kiss again. It would be wrong."

"The heck you can't. You're not locked into a script. You can kiss and do whatever else you want to do together. You're no longer his nurse. In fact, you're no longer a nurse period. You run a daycare center. So kiss away, sister."

"But I'm afraid."

"Of what?"

"Caring too much."

"You lost that battle a long time ago where Jack is involved. From the moment he came into your life, you had a thing for him. If he feels the same, don't throw it away."

Maybe Laura was right, Zara thought after they'd finished talking. She set the alarm clock for thirty minutes and crawled under the covers.

Jack removed his prosthetic legs and lay down. He hadn't realized just how tired he was until he hit the bed. He glanced at the Cause a Ripple gift set sitting on the dresser and felt for the stone in his pocket. He smiled thinking about the kiss. Everything about it was perfect.

Her lips had felt silky soft. He hoped to feel them again but didn't want to pressure her. And he wondered if she liked him or pitied him. He thought it was the former, but doubts crept into his mind when he was alone.

Could there ever be more between them, he wondered. Why would she want him? A guy with fake legs. A guy who looked like he was walking on poles. Still, he felt the urgency in their kiss, and he knew there was something there. He was ready to take a chance, but he wasn't sure Zara was.

In the six months since he'd last seen her, so much had happened. Her mom had died, and Zara had taken over her mom's daycare. She'd launched her Cause a Ripple website, and it was beginning to gain attention from national media. Her dreams were coming true, and Jack wondered if there was a place for him in those dreams.

He planned to start college in a few months, taking online courses at first. He figured he'd stay in Bethesda, near the medical center, so he'd be close if he needed adjustments to his prostheses or additional therapy. Zara, who was now living in Alexandria, wouldn't be that far away. A relationship would be possible, if she was game. But he didn't want to push too fast too soon. Besides, he had a long journey ahead of him, and it didn't seem right to ask her to walk by his side. Or to carry him.

Jack fell asleep clutching the heart-shaped stone Zara had given him so long ago. He wished she was there. He wanted to hold her. He could smell her hair. Feel her curls tickle his neck as she laid her head on his shoulder.

An hour later, Jack jerked awake. He squirmed closer to his nightstand so he could answer the phone. "Hello."

"Wake up, sleepy head!"

"Ugh! It's that time already?"

Zara laughed. "Afraid so. But if you're too tired and you want to skip going to see the Empire State Building, that's okay."

"Are you kidding? I wouldn't miss seeing that with you for anything."

"I wonder what color the building will be."

"Color?" Jack asked.

"Yeah. They light the upper floors. It's pretty cool, actually. Depending on the season—it's blue and white for Hanukkah, red and green for Christmas, yellow and white for spring. You get the idea."

"Pity the guys who have to change the lenses on the floodlights."

"Oh, they don't. Not anymore," Zara explained. "They use computerized LEDs, and it's all controlled from a computer console."

Jack laughed. "Maybe you should be a tour guide."

"Maybe I should."

They laughed.

"How about we meet at the bar downstairs in forty-five minutes," Zara said. "Is that enough time?"

"Perfect," Jack said. "See you then."

Jack lingered in bed another five minutes before forcing himself to get up. He turned on the TV to check the weather. After a quick shower and shave, he went down to the bar. He sat facing the door so he could see Zara when she arrived.

The bartender walked over. "Can I get you something?"

Jack looked at the beers on draft. "I'll take a Yuengling."

The bartender grabbed a glass from the freezer behind the bar and held it under the tap, tilting it as he filled it. He slid the draft in front of Jack. "Can I ask you something?"

"Sure." Jack picked up the beer and took a sip.

"How'd it happen? The legs, I mean."

Jack licked his lips. "Roadside bomb."

"In Afghanistan?"

Jack nodded, and their conversation was cut short when he spotted Zara. He waved, and she walked over and slid onto the stool next to him. Jack couldn't help but notice how every man in the bar turned to watch her. He didn't blame them. Zara was a natural beauty, stunning without even trying.

"I hope you weren't waiting long," Zara said.

Jack waved his hand. "Only a few minutes."

Zara ordered an old-fashioned cocktail.

Jack shook his head. "Now, that's a first. Never been with a girl who ordered an old-fashioned before."

Zara shrugged. "It's my dad's drink of choice, so I've come to like it."

"Nate liked old-fashions too," Jack said.

"Nate?"

Jack reached for the bowl of peanuts. "He was my best friend. He died in the explosion."

Zara knew Jack's best friend had been a gunner and that he'd died in the same explosion, but she hadn't known his name. And yet, it sounded vaguely familiar. But as soon as Jack explained, Zara remembered where she'd heard it before. Jack had cried out Nate's name during his nightmares.

The bartender put the drink in front of Zara, and she picked up the maraschino cherry used as a garnish and offered it to Jack. Jack held up his hand. "I don't like them," he said.

Zara stuck it in her mouth and pulled off the stem, laying it on a napkin. "I never met anyone who didn't like cherries."

Jack held up his finger. "I have a good reason. I had a cherry tree in my backyard, and one summer, Nate and I cooked up this plan to make a quick buck. Instead of picking cherries off the tree, we picked them off the ground. Most of them weren't fit to eat. But we concealed the rotten cherries by topping the box off with good ones. But we didn't count on our neighbor calling my mom when she discovered she'd been had."

Zara laughed. "So what happened?"

"Mom made us pick twice the number of boxes of cherries we sold, and everyone got double what they bought. So Mrs. Swan, who bought two, got four. We picked those cherries all day."

Zara propped her elbow on the bar and rested her chin on her fist. "Did you have to give back the money?"

"We couldn't," Jack said. "We'd already spent it. As soon as we got the money, we took off for the store and loaded up on candy."

"Guess you never did that again!"

Jack smiled. "Never. And I was so sick of picking cherries that to this day I can't even eat one."

Zara sipped her drink. "That's a great story."

Jack nodded. "It's one I'll have to tell Nate's son when he's older."

Jack explained that Nate had died before his son was born. He also told her about the four-leaf clover and the promise he'd made Nate.

"When are you going to visit?" Zara asked.

"Not sure. Hopefully soon."

"Well, if you want company, I'll go."

Jack looked at Zara. "You'd really do that?"

"Sure. I know it'll probably be tough. Might be good to have a friend along."

"Thanks," Jack said. "Nate's family has always been good to me. Ever since the accident, I haven't been able to face them. I got some letters from his mom, and his sisters have called, but I just couldn't talk to them. I'd give anything if Nate were here instead of me."

Zara reached over and touched Jack's hand. "Stop blaming yourself, Jack. That's the last thing Nate would've wanted."

Jack rubbed his neck. "But he should be here. Not me. He's the one who has a kid counting on him. Me? I don't have anyone. No one would've missed me if I'd been the one dead in the dirt."

Zara rubbed Jack's arm. "That's not true. I'm sure a lot of people would've missed you. I'm not going to be one of those people who say things happen for a reason. I know that's not what you want to hear. I didn't want to hear that either after Johnny and Mom died. But I have to believe it's in God's hands, that He has a plan. And, yeah, I might not understand it or agree with it. It might make me angry. But I've got to trust that He knows what He's doing. Otherwise, our lives are just one mess after another without any real purpose. Each of us has a purpose—we just need to find it."

Jack nodded. "And have you found yours with the stones?"

Zara shifted in her seat. "I think so. I finally feel like I'm doing what I'm meant to be doing. Believe me, if someone had told me I'd be starting a foundation and would come up with a stone ministry to recognize others, I would've laughed. But it feels right. *So* right. And I can't ignore that little voice inside of me telling me to continue on despite whatever obstacles I might face."

Jack finished his beer. "But if something's meant to be, why's it so hard?"

Zara sighed. "That's a good question. Maybe it's to make us appreciate the accomplishment more. If something's easy, do we appreciate it as much as if it had taken no effort? Think of how hard you've had to work to get where you are today. You survived a boatload of surgeries. Endured hours of physical therapy. Fought giving up when it would've been easier to wallow in self-pity. Instead, you found the courage and the strength to move on, overcoming one obstacle after another. There's a reason why you're here, Jack. You just have to find it."

They finished their drinks, hailed a taxi, and headed for the Empire State Building.

"Oh, look," Zara said as they pulled up. "It's lit up in red, white, and blue."

"Maybe it's for Flag Day," Jack said.

"I bet you're right," Zara said. "I hadn't even thought of that."

When they entered the building, Jack bought express tickets. "No way am I going to wait in line."

Zara pulled out her wallet. "At least let me pay for mine."

"No," Jack said. "My treat."

Zara stuffed her wallet back inside her purse. "Well, okay. Thank you."

They took the elevator to the top floor and walked out into the observatory. They looked down over the glittery skyscrapers.

"It's like a sea of fireflies, all lit at the same time," Zara said. "It takes my breath away. I visited once during the day, which was nice because I could see landmarks. But there's just something magical about being up here at night."

Jack put his arms around Zara, hoping she wouldn't pull away. She didn't.

Jack pointed to a plane in the distance. "When I was a boy and I'd see planes in the sky, I'd always imagine I was onboard."

Zara twirled around and faced him. "Where did you imagine you were going?"

"Different places." Jack brushed Zara's curls off her face. "Sometimes I imagined I was going to Disney World. Other times, to exotic places like Bora Bora. I wanted to be anywhere but where I was."

"And where was that?" Zara asked.

"In Hell."

Zara brushed Jack's arm. "Was growing up that bad?"

"It was tough being illegitimate in a small town where you were judged by your lineage and what church you attended."

Zara touched Jack's cheek. "I'm sorry. It sounds like you had a pretty crummy life when you were a kid."

"It only got better as an adult when I could make my own choices. Be independent. I thought Afghanistan took that from me. Until you pushed me to believe in myself again."

CHAPTER TWENTY-ONE

Zara insisted on walking Jack to his room. "I'm so glad you bought those express passes or we'd still be standing in line! Thanks for spending the day with me. I had a great time."

"Me too." Jacked pulled out his room key and turned to face Zara. "So what happens next? We both go home tomorrow. What then?"

Zara figured this conversation would come sooner or later. She'd sensed on the taxi ride back to the hotel that Jack wanted to say something. It wasn't the kind of conversation that took a minute in a hotel hallway.

"It might be better to talk in your room," Zara said.

"Sure." Jack slid his card into the slot and opened the door.

Zara followed Jack inside, and they sat on the edge of his bed. "What do you want to happen?" Zara asked.

"I know what I don't want to happen. I don't want you to walk out of my life again. I want to keep seeing you."

"I like you, Jack, I do. But I need to make sure that I fix myself before getting involved with someone."

"What's there to fix? You're perfect."

"I'm definitely not perfect. I want to do so much more with Cause a Ripple. I have an interview with a reporter tomorrow before I leave to go home."

Jack shifted so that his body was angled toward her. "That's great. Getting press should help."

"Yeah. And then I need to get home and take care of Kids Academy. I can't let what Mom built collapse."

"I'm sure you won't."

"So I'm not sure I have time for more in my life right now."

Jack reached for Zara's hand. "I'm not asking for much time, just a little. I just have to know that when I go back, I'll see you again. We can go out to dinner or just sit and talk. I don't care. I just want to be with you."

Zara stared into his dark, gorgeous eyes. "I want to be with you too, but I'm scared."

"Of what?"

"Of feeling too much, caring too much. And it still bothers me that I was your nurse."

"Quit making excuses, Zara. Yes, you were my nurse. That's how we met and what brought us together. Nothing can change that. But you're not my nurse anymore. You talk about Cause a Ripple. But don't you see that it's what brought us together? You wouldn't have been in New York if it hadn't been for that. And I wouldn't have been in New York if it hadn't been for you."

Jack pulled the heart-shaped stone Zara had given him out of his pocket. He held it up. "This stone is what got me through everything. I'd broken it once, and I never thought I'd be able to put it back together. But I did. This stone gave me hope when I had none. Light when I only saw darkness. You can't begin to imagine the difference you've made in my life. Whenever I felt defeated, I'd clutch this stone and remember. You want to talk about causing ripples? Well, you created a tidal wave in my life. And I'm not going to let you walk out of it again. I don't know how we'll end up, but I know we have to try."

Tears pooled in Zara's eyes, and her chin trembled. "I don't want to disappoint you or hurt you."

"Then don't walk away," Jack said. "Stay and take a chance. I'm willing. I'm more than willing. I just want to hold you and never let you go."

"Then hold me. Just hold me."

Jack wrapped his arm around her, pulling her in close. They talked for what seemed like hours and eventually fell asleep.

Zara woke up before Jack and went back to her room, but not before leaving him a note. The last thing she wanted was for him to feel as if she was abandoning him.

She'd never been happier. She felt safe in his arms, and she wondered if he desired her as much as she did him. He hadn't pushed for more than kissing, and so Zara followed his lead. But deep inside, she desired him more than she'd ever desired any man. She wanted to be with him, completely. And she wondered if he felt the same way.

Jack woke up and rolled over on his side, expecting to see Zara. His heart sank when she wasn't there. But he picked up the note she'd left on the pillow and read it.

Dear Jack,

Thank you for holding me. I loved being in your arms and hope to find myself in them again. I had to go shower and get ready for my interview, but I'll call you later today. This isn't the end. It's a new beginning. At least that's what I'm hoping for.

Love, Zara

Jack punched the air with his fist and shouted, "Yeah!" He kissed the letter and folded it. He planned to keep it forever. He picked up his cell phone and sent her a text.

I loved holding you. Good luck today.

She texted back.

Thanks. I'll call you later. Have a safe flight.

By the time Jack showered and checked out, Zara was already gone. He took a cab to the airport. While he waited at the gate, he tried reading the newspaper he'd bought, but he couldn't get her out of his mind. For a split second, he thought he saw her out of the corner of his eye, but the blonde curly hair belonged to a woman twice Zara's size.

Jack smiled as he thought about holding Zara, his arm around her waist and her curls tickling his nose. He wondered what being with her would be like. He desperately wanted to find out. What if he turned her off? What if he couldn't be the man he once was? What if things no longer worked the way they once did?

He was a knot of doubts and fears. He hadn't talked to Tom about being with a woman. Maybe he should. After all, it obviously worked out for Tom. Surely, he could advise Jack in the intimacy department.

Zara sat across from the reporter in a small conference room at the newspaper's office in lower Manhattan. Her hands were sweaty. She hadn't realized how nervous she was. It was the first time she'd been interviewed by someone other than a potential employer.

The reporter, Ellen McFadden, had learned about Zara while covering the race in Central Park. She pulled out a small tape recorder. "Do you mind if I record our interview?"

Zara shook her head. "Can I read the article before it's published?"

Ellen smiled. "Sorry, we don't do that. But I can call you and go over the general gist of the story. And, of course, double check all facts."

Zara sighed. She was concerned she'd sound stupid.

"Don't worry," Ellen said. "I'll make this as painless as possible." She pulled out a notebook and pen and turned on the tape recorder. "So, tell me about the inspiration behind Cause a Ripple."

Zara explained the church sermon and how she couldn't get it out of her mind.

"So you pulled off the highway to get gas and heard the church bells?" Ellen asked.

"Yes. And it was strange, but I had an overwhelming urge to visit the church."

"And you'd never been to this church before?"

"Correct. I asked the clerk at the gas station for directions."

"So you ended up in an unfamiliar church, listening to a minister you'd never met before giving a sermon you weren't expecting to hear?"

"Exactly, and the sermon blew me away. I couldn't stop thinking about the metaphor, about how our actions impact others."

"So when did your pebble of an idea become something more?" Ellen stressed the word pebble as if she needed to alert Zara to the pun.

"As I said, I couldn't stop thinking about it. Then I went into my brother's room when I was visiting my parents. He was a Marine sergeant and was killed in Afghanistan."

"Excuse me," Ellen said. "How did he die?"

Zara took a deep breath. "He was a bomb disposal expert and stepped on an IED."

"Oh," Ellen said. "I'm sorry."

Zara nodded. She told her all about Johnny, and how close they were, and how she found the bag of stones in his nightstand drawer, surely a sign she was doing exactly what she was destined to do.

"Looking over your bio, I see you were a nurse at Walter Reed. Are you still working there?"

"No." Zara explained, "After Johnny died, I left my job. I was caring for wounded veterans, and I needed some time away. So I lived in Florida for about six months. And I couldn't get the sermon and the stone idea out of my mind. While I was there, I worked on the project."

"What has been the most challenging part of the project?"

Zara laughed. "That's easy. Setting up the foundation was a nightmare. The set-up and tax-filing fees were crazy expensive. I didn't think it would happen, because I just didn't have the money. But then the lawyer who was working with me—and by the way, he had donated his time—received an anonymous donation."

Ellen smiled. "So in a sense, the foundation, or ripple if you will, was the result of the anonymous donation, or stone, being thrown into the water."

"Precisely," Zara said. "And now the foundation will hopefully create ripples in the lives of others."

Ellen held up the card with the Cause a Ripple logo on it. "I love your design. Was that hard to find?"

"Not really," Zara said. "I had an amazing graphic artist who helped make my vision come to life."

"Did you know any of the wounded veterans who raced in Central Park that you gave stones to?"

"As a matter of fact, I did. One racer was a former patient."

Ellen smiled. "That must've been a surprise."

Zara nodded. "It was. I hadn't seen him since I left Walter Reed, and I didn't know he was a participant until his name was called at the awards banquet."

Zara felt her face heat up. She tried to conceal her feelings for Jack, but she figured Ellen saw there was something more there because she continued on that line of questioning.

"So you and…?"

"Jack." Zara fidgeted in her chair.

"Last name?" Ellen asked.

"Quinlan."

"So you and Jack Quinlan reconnected at the banquet?" Ellen said.

Zara smiled. "Yes. When I left Walter Reed, he didn't even have his stubbies. Now he's walking on prosthetic legs and racing a handcycle."

"So he's come a long way?"

Zara nodded. "All of the race participants have." She hoped that by bringing up the other racers it would lead the reporter to another line of questions.

It worked. "What's it like to see these wounded soldiers running marathons and participating in other sports after losing arms and legs?"

"It's amazing. They're all amazing. They have so much determination. They don't see themselves as victims. They don't focus on what they've lost, but on what they have, and when they go out there and handcycle, or run, or climb a mountain, or sky dive, or swim, they're showing others like them that their life isn't over, but beginning again. Yes, things will be different, but life can still be good."

Zara took a deep breath. She hadn't expected to go on like that, but she was glad she had.

"Is there anything else I didn't ask that you think I should know?"

"I think you've been very thorough," Zara said. "But if I think of anything, I'll let you know." She handed her a business card. "And if you have any questions, don't hesitate to call me."

Ellen turned off the tape recorder and held out her hand to shake Zara's. "Thank you for coming by. And I wish you luck with your foundation. You're doing a great thing, and you're helping a lot of people."

Zara smiled and followed Ellen to the front door, where she hailed a taxi and headed for the airport.

CHAPTER TWENTY-TWO

Jack was unpacking his suitcase when he heard the doorbell. It was Tom.

"I just wanted to stop over and congratulate you on the race. You did it, man!" He high-fived Jack.

Jack smiled. "Thanks! Do you have a minute? I wanted to ask you something."

Tom pulled out a chair and sat across from Jack. "Everything okay, Jack? I can tell by the look on your face something's bothering you."

Jack nodded. "Remember when I asked you about being intimate?"

Tom sat up straighter. "Yeah, you asked how it was, and I told you great but different. Why? Are you figuring on getting intimate soon?"

Jack laughed. "Zara and I—"

"Whoa! Back up. Zara as in your nurse, Zara?"

"Former nurse," Jack said. "And, no, our relationship hasn't progressed beyond kissing and hugging. But I'd like it to."

Tom leaned forward. "Maybe you better start at the beginning."

Jack started the story with the banquet and ended it with him holding Zara and falling asleep wrapped in each other's arms.

"But I wanted to please her, you know, in other ways, but I was a little afraid."

"What you're feeling is completely normal," Tom said. "I'll be honest, it is different."

Tom advised Jack on the intricacies of having a physical relationship.

"This is probably going to sound like a stupid question, but do I remove my legs?"

"First, no question is dumb," Tom said. "Second, I would in bed, definitely. And using pillows for support can help."

Jack nodded. "I guess I'm scared of being rejected. I mean, you know Zara. The woman's gorgeous. I sense that she cares for me as much as I care for her. But why would she want me when she could have anyone out there with four limbs?"

"It's normal to fear rejection," Tom said. "I worried about that too. I worried Jen would no longer find me attractive and that she'd be turned off when I removed my prostheses in bed. But she wasn't. In fact, intimacy is a very special part of our relationship, just as it was before the amputations."

"But it was different for you guys because you were a couple before the accident."

"True," Tom said. "But she could've been repulsed and unable to handle it. In your case, Zara didn't know you before the accident, so you'd be developing an intimate relationship with someone who has never seen you any other way. This might be better because you're developing the relationship with the amputations right up front."

"Guess I never thought about that," Jack said.

"Plus," Tom said, "Zara's a nurse. And she's a nurse who just happens to have cared for wounded veterans missing limbs, including you. My guess is she's aware of your doubts, and fears, and how you're struggling with your body image. Not because you're acting a certain way, but because of her experience and training. If your relationship progresses to that point, I bet she makes it very comfortable for you. It all comes down to insecurities, Jack. And it's just something you'll need to work through."

Jack sighed. "Yeah, it's tough, you know. Especially since we live in a culture obsessed with physical perfection and beauty."

"Amen, brother. Just give things time. If Zara's the right one, it won't be because of your condition, but because of the person you are as a whole."

Zara texted Jack after she got through airport security and was at the gate.

At airport. Interview went well. Call you later.

Jack texted back a smiley face emoticon.

Can't wait. Have a good flight.

After she texted Jack, she texted Laura and Stacey to let them know about the interview and that she'd call them later. She ended up on the plane sitting beside a woman headed to visit her daughter. Zara had planned on taking a nap, but Ingrid, who hated flying, kept talking. Zara figured talking probably helped Ingrid because it kept her mind off the flight, so she listened and commented when she could.

Ingrid reminded Zara of her mother, only twenty years older. She had white hair, and she wore it in a bun. She was dressed in stylish tan pants and a coral floral blouse. And her nails were professionally manicured with rose-colored nail polish.

Zara learned Ingrid was from Germany and that she'd met her husband while he was in the military. They had two sons and a daughter. Her husband had died in a car accident when he was in his fifties, the result of driving too fast and losing control of his car on a slick road.

Ingrid lowered her voice. "I'm almost embarrassed to tell you this."

Zara leaned in closer and listened as Ingrid shared her story of becoming addicted to gambling after her husband died.

"I lost my home and the respect of my children," Ingrid explained. "I gambled away all of the insurance money I received after his death. I was penniless. But I started going to Gamblers Anonymous meetings, and I struggled for a long time. Eventually, my kids forgave me and I started running the meetings, helping others who were where I'd been."

Zara smiled. She always kept a Cause a Ripple stone in her purse for times like this. She'd give them to people who inspired her, who were making a difference in other people's lives, like Ingrid.

Zara reached into her purse and pulled out the stone. She turned to Ingrid and explained the stone and the sermon that had inspired it. "So I want you to have this as a reminder of your strength and the impact you've had on others."

Ingrid held up her hand. "But I lost everything."

Zara nodded. "Yes, and you struggled and took perhaps your greatest weakness and turned it around to become a strength to help others."

Ingrid's blue eyes sparkled. She took the stone and held it to her heart. "I will treasure this always. Thank you."

Zara gave Ingrid a business card with her e-mail address on it. "Drop me a note every now and then and tell me how you're doing."

Ingrid patted Zara's arm. "I will, sweetie."

Zara listened as Ingrid's life story unfurled. Her bout with breast cancer. Her grandson who was studying to be a doctor. Her daughter who couldn't have a child of her own and adopted two girls from China. By the end of the flight, Zara felt as if she'd known Ingrid for years instead of for hours.

Zara's dad was waiting for her in the baggage claim area. She saw him as soon as she exited the escalator. He wrapped his arms around her and kissed her cheek. "How's my favorite girl?"

Zara hugged him back. "Great, Dad. Although I'm nervous about the newspaper interview. I hope I didn't sound stupid."

"I'm sure you sounded fine. And, who knows, maybe the press will help get Cause a Ripple known. I'm so proud of what you've done with it so far. And your mother would be too."

Zara knew how much her dad missed her mom, and she worried if he'd be all right after she moved into her own place. Of course, he told her she could live with him for as long as she wanted. There was plenty of room. It was only him in the four-bedroom, two-bathroom house. But Zara wanted her own place. And she figured her dad would eventually downsize into a condo, something her parents had been thinking about before her mom died.

"Thanks," Zara said, and she told him about Jack.

"Guess you were surprised when you saw him."

"Yeah. You could say that. When I resigned from the medical center, he wasn't even wearing stubbies." Zara bit her lower lip and stared into the distance.

"I know that look. Your mother had that same look when she was holding something back. Go ahead. Out with it."

Zara and her dad had always been close. Still, she wondered how much to tell him. She waited until they retrieved her luggage and were headed home.

"Okay. We're on the highway. Don't make your old man wait any longer. Out with it."

Zara breathed in deeply and exhaled slowly. "The day after the banquet, we went sightseeing. We went to the 9/11 Memorial and the Empire State Building."

"And you like him, right?" her dad asked.

"You always cut to the chase, don't you, Dad?"

He shrugged and smiled.

"Of course I like him."

"That's not what I meant by like," her dad said. "I meant 'like' as in you're attracted to him, would like to date him."

Zara nodded. "Yes. And I think he likes me."

"You think?"

Zara shifted in her seat. "Okay. Yes. He likes me too. A lot."

"Well, then. What are you waiting for? Life's too short, Zara. We both know that."

Zara smiled. "It's not that simple."

Zara's dad stopped at the red light. He looked over at her. "It is if you want it to be. Don't make things so complicated, Zara. If you like this guy and enjoy spending time with him, why in the world would you not? We only get one shot at this life. Make it a good one. I want my little girl to find someone special. To be happy. You're never going to find someone special if you never take chances. It's about time you take your foot off of first base and head toward second. Maybe eventually you'll make it to home plate."

Zara laughed. "You and your baseball metaphors. But, thanks, Dad. I'll think about what you said. I love you."

The light turned green, and the driver behind them honked his horn. Her dad jerked to attention. He pulled ahead and reached over and touched Zara's hand. "I love you. I want you to be happy. That's all I've ever wanted. I want a man who will make you happy, who will love you in both good and bad times. And whoever that guy turns out to be, I know he has to be really special because my girl's special."

Later that night, Zara called Jack. She told him about the interview and how his name came up.

"I know," Jack said.

"What do you mean, you know?"

"The reporter. What's her name?"

"Ellen."

"Yeah, Ellen called me. She wanted to talk with one of the racers who'd received a stone. You know, get their thoughts for the story. She said she'd heard from you that I'd been your patient."

"Oh, I'm so sorry, Jack. I had no idea she'd call you. If I knew, I would've given you a heads up."

"I'm glad she did," Jack said. "It gave me a chance to tell her what a great person you are."

"Did you tell her anything else?"

"Like what?" Jack asked.

"Oh, I don't know. Like about the other stone. The first stone I gave you. Did you say anything about that?"

"You mean how the heart-shaped stone breaking mirrored my heart breaking when I'd learned you'd left?" Jack teased.

"Stop it," Zara said.

"No, I didn't say anything you wouldn't have wanted me to say. What you're doing is amazing. You're amazing. That's what I told her."

"Thanks."

"Does that mean I can see you again? How about dinner or something? I'll come there."

"Actually," Zara said. "I'm going to Laura's next weekend to see her new place. Maybe we can grab dinner on Saturday?"

"Perfect," Jack said. "There's a little Italian place I found that I think you'd love."

"Then it's a date."

Zara called Laura after she got off the phone with Jack and gave her the lowdown.

"So you were in bed beside him, but nothing happened."

"We kissed."

"Other than that. Nothing?"

"Well, I wanted to. And I think he wanted to. But we didn't. And it killed me. I'd never wanted to be with a guy as much as I want to be with Jack. And I still feel a little weird about it since he was my patient. Somehow it still seems wrong."

"Well, get over that, sister. He's not your patient. In fact, you're not even a nurse anymore. You're a businesswoman, and you own a wildly successful daycare center."

"I know. I know. I just need time. I mean, everything is happening so fast. I hadn't seen Jack since I left the medical center, and he shows up out of the blue at a banquet in New York City." She sighed. "It's crazy. I mean, when I heard his name announced, I couldn't believe it. And then when I saw him, all those old feelings resurfaced."

"So when are you going to see him again?"

"Next weekend."

"But you're coming here."

"Right. I'll come Friday and go out to dinner with Jack Saturday night."

"We could do dinner here on Saturday night. Or do you want him all to yourself?"

"Sort of. I mean, there's so much we need to learn about each other yet. We're off to a great start, but I'd like to know him better before I introduce him to all my friends. Are you mad?"

"Of course not. But you know I have to ask it because, well, I'm your best friend. Do you like him or pity him?"

Zara sighed. "That's a fair question, one I've asked myself. And while I have empathy for Jack and others like him, what I'm feeling is more than that. When I was in Florida, I had plenty of opportunities to date. I never did. I couldn't stop thinking about Jack. And then when he came back into my life unexpectedly, well, it's like it was meant to be."

"Then go for it, girlfriend. I'm happy for you. And for Jack. You both deserve happiness."

CHAPTER TWENTY-THREE

"I have one more leg than you, and you still beat me every time," said Sam after racing Jack.

Jack walked off the track to get his water bottle. "Good race, Sam."

Sam wiped the sweat off his face with a towel. "I think you get faster every day."

Jack laughed. "I know you do. It's getting harder and harder to beat you."

"So how did it go with Zara?"

Jack hadn't spoken to Sam since he'd returned from New York, and he gave him the highlights.

"You really like her, don't you?"

Jack nodded. "I never met anyone quite like her."

"Does she feel the same way?"

Jack shrugged. "I think so. Not sure if she likes me as much as I like her, but we'll see. She's coming next weekend."

Sam's eyes widened. "Well, that's a good sign. She must like you if she's coming to see you."

"She's actually coming to see her girlfriend who lives here. But we're going out Saturday night. I was going to take her to that new Italian place on the corner of Main and Maple."

"Good choice," Sam said.

"What about you? Anything more from that former classmate you reconnected with online?"

"We've been texting," Sam said. "She asked me if I was going to our tenth class reunion."

"Are you?"

"I wasn't going to, but I'm reconsidering. She said she was going."

"Might be a great opportunity to meet up in person. It's a great excuse, and if you don't hit it off, there'll be plenty of other people to talk to."

"True," Sam said. "I just don't want everyone to pity me. I don't want them to look at me and think, 'Poor Sam, and he used to be such a great athlete. Now look at him.'"

"You never told me you played sports in school."

Sam shrugged. "Well, I did. Baseball was my best sport."

"If you want to throw ball sometime, let me know."

"Can't." Sam wiggled his residual limb. "I lost my throwing arm."

"And you're going to let that stop you?" Jack pointed to Sam's good arm. "The Sam I know would learn to throw with his other arm.

When Zara walked into the kitchen, her dad was on his second cup of coffee. Zara looked at her mom's chair. "I miss her so much."

Her dad nodded. "Me too. But she'd be so proud of you. Speaking of which." He picked up his iPad. "Here's the story in the *Times*."

Zara's hand flew to her chest. "Omigosh! How is it? Do I sound dumb? The reporter never called to go over the story."

Zara's dad held up his hand. "Don't worry. It's a great article, and I bet it creates a few ripples of its own."

Zara sat down and read the story. She smiled when she read Jack's comments. *It's a reminder not only of the differences I've made but of those I can make. I keep it with me always.*

"The man in that article—is that him?"

Zara nodded.

"He sounds like a nice young man. And, see, the article was good. You didn't sound dumb at all."

Zara hugged her dad and walked over to the counter to get a cup of coffee. He followed and refilled his mug.

"Zara, Aunt Cindy has offered to go through your mom's things. I told her I'd ask you."

"I want to do it."

"Are you sure?"

Zara sat back down. "Yes. I figured I'd donate the clothes to the program that helps women get back on their feet."

"Sounds like a great idea."

Zara pulled out her cell phone to check her e-mail. She received notice through her website that she'd made a sale. She'd sold one hundred stones. Her eyes widened, and she gasped.

"Everything okay, sweetie?"

"I had some sales," she said. "Someone bought a hundred stones. I have another order for fifteen. Guess I know what I'll be doing later—packaging stones."

"I'll help," her dad said. "We can do it together."

"Thanks, Dad. And here's an e-mail from Ingrid's daughter, the woman I told you I met on the plane."

"The woman who gambled all of her money away?"

"Yes. Listen to this. 'Dear Zara, Mother showed me the stone you gave her. I love the idea of giving stones as a way of recognizing the impact we have on others. I bought fifteen to give to my staff. Thank you for reaching out to mother, and I wish you luck with Cause a Ripple. Best, Becky.'"

"That's a nice note," her dad said. "I'm so proud of you. How about I pick up some Chinese on the way home from work? We can eat and put together the gift sets."

"Sounds great, Dad."

Zara was getting ready to leave for work when Stacey called.

"Sorry I missed your call last night," Stacey said. "After work, I came home and crashed. I didn't wake up until this morning."

Zara gave her the cliff notes of New York and her time with Jack. "And I had an interview with a reporter from the Times."

"Which one?"

"Ellen McFadden."

"Oh, I love her stuff. As soon as we get off the phone, I'm going to read it."

"And I sold more than a hundred stones overnight."

"See, I told you Cause a Ripple was going to be a hit."

Zara laughed. "Well, it takes more than one hit to win a game, but it's off to a good start. I just hope I can keep it going and growing. I want to make sure that the core of the idea is the driving force. To recognize the good and great things about others and to inspire."

"Well, you inspire me," Stacey said. "I gotta run or I'll be late for work. Talk to you later."

By the time Zara got to work, the center was alive with kids. Her office assistant, Trudy, handed her a slip of paper. "You've had several calls this morning already, including a reporter from the local paper. They want to do a story about the stones."

"They must have read about it in the *Times*."

"Are you still planning to visit the four- and five-year-old classrooms today for observation?"

"Yes," Zara said. "I'll visit one in the morning and one after lunch."

Zara went to her office and pulled out her cell phone to check her messages. She had received a text from Laura, congratulating her on the article.

Zara was happier than she'd been in a long time. She'd read somewhere that people who were living their purpose added years to their lives and life to their years, and she believed that with all her heart.

After tackling the mountain of paperwork on her desk and returning several calls, it was time to visit Miss Emily's classroom. She walked down the hall, turned the corner, and walked into the room. Colorful posters covered the walls, and a train of alphabet cards ran across the front of the classroom, inches from the ceiling.

She watched the children play and noticed a little boy by himself. Then she saw a girl walk over to him, black braids bouncing as she went. "Do you want to color?" She held out a coloring book and crayons. He nodded, and they sat at a nearby table.

Zara walked over and knelt beside the girl. "It was very nice of you to ask him to color."

The little girl smiled, and her brown eyes widened.

Zara enjoyed visiting the classrooms, and she made a point of recognizing the children when they did something nice. She noticed that the more good things she recognized the more ripples she created. Pointing them out encouraged even more. She loved the idea of teaching them at a young age they could make a difference.

During her afternoon classroom visit, a photographer from the local newspaper came to take photos and shoot a video of her interacting with the children. Later, she sat down with the reporter, Sarah Smith. Sarah asked many of the same questions the other reporter had asked, but she delved more deeply into her formative years. After all, this was the town where Zara grew up, went to school and church. She was one of their own.

"Why did you return to the area?" Sarah asked.

"After my mother died, I decided to take over the daycare center. I loved the idea of having an impact on children, teaching them at a young age they can make a difference through their actions."

"So it's sort of like causing ripples?"

Zara smiled. "Precisely. And when I praise them for politeness, or sharing, or singing, or drawing, or playing well, or trying hard, or helping, I can see their faces light up."

By the time Zara had finished the interview, she was exhausted. She was glad her dad suggested picking up Chinese food because the last thing she wanted to do was cook. Besides, she had a lot of stone gift sets to put together.

CHAPTER TWENTY-FOUR

Jack walked into the rehab gym looking for Pete. He found him at the parallel bars, working with a woman who'd just gotten her stubbies. Jack watched as she took her first steps. When she got to the end, everyone clapped. Jack shouted, "Way to go!"

Pete looked up and waved. "What are you doing here?"

Jack walked over. "I had to see your pretty face."

Pete laughed. "Ashley, this is Jack. Jack, meet Ashley."

Jack and Ashley shook hands. "You're the marathon man Pete told me about."

Jack chuckled. "Marathon Man? Well, I'm getting there. Just did my first 5K."

"Handcycle or did you run on your legs?" Ashley asked.

Jack made a pedal motion with his hands. "Handcycle. But I'd definitely like to try running on my legs."

Ashley wiped the sweat off her face with her towel. "I was thinking about trying handcycling, but then I decided to get into swimming. I swam on my high school team. It's been great getting back into the water."

"Well, if you like to swim and cycle, you could train for a triathlon," Jack said. "How were you injured?"

"IED. I was on a clearance mission. We'd just taken out sixteen IEDs. I found one more the hard way."

Jack pointed to Pete. "Listen to this guy. He'll take good care of you."

"How about a ten-minute break?" Pete handed Ashley a bottle of water.

Ashley turned to Jack. "Thanks for coming. This is the first break Pete's given me today."

Jack nodded. "He's definitely tough, but he'll get you on those new legs in no time. Trust him."

"I will. You're living proof of Pete's magic."

"Oh, stop it, you two," Pete said. "You're embarrassing me."

Pete and Jack walked out of the gym and found two chairs in the lounge.

"So, how's it really going, Jack?" Pete said.

"Good. I saw her."

"Saw who?"

"Zara."

Pete's eyebrows arched. "Now, there's a name I haven't heard for a while. How's she doing?"

"Great. We met at the banquet following the race in New York. She presented Cause a Ripple stones at the banquet."

"What are they?"

Jack explained the stones. "And she has a website where she sells them and a nonprofit foundation she's established that benefits various charities. The *Times* did an article about her after the race. They even interviewed me."

"Wow, good for her. It sounds like everything is finally coming together."

Jack explained the rest of the story, how they spent the day together sightseeing in New York and how she planned to visit in a few days. "She's coming to see her best friend, Laura. I guess she has a new place. But we're going out Saturday night."

"So are you guys a thing?"

Jack shook his head. "But I'd sure like to be."

Pete looked at his watch. "I'd better get back to Ashley. It was great seeing you, Jack."

"It was great seeing you too, Pete. And, Pete, thanks."

Pete smiled. "For what?"

"For not giving up on me."

Pete nodded and turned toward the rehab gym. Jack turned toward his prosthetist's office.

Lee saw Jack as soon as he walked in and waved him over to where he was working. They shook hands. "How are the legs?"

"Good."

"Let's have a look." Lee checked his legs. "The knees are working well?"

"They're amazing. If I had to get injured, I'm glad it was at a time when we have all this amazing technology."

Lee finished checking Jack's legs and stood up. "So, I heard you did a 5K."

Jack flashed a 1,000-watt smile. "One of the best things about the race was inspiring others, showing them there's life after losing your limbs."

"Sounds like a speech we had to give you a time or two."

Jack laughed. "You're right. I guess we all get there sooner or later, some a little later than others. I want to become a peer counselor, like Tom. Help others the way he helped me."

Lee smiled. "Then I'm sure you will. If there's one thing I've come to know through working with you, it's that you say what you mean and do what you say."

"I hope that's a good thing."

"It's a very good thing.

Zara smelled the Chinese food as soon as she walked into the house.

"Hi, sweetie." Her dad got plates from the cabinet. "How was your day?"

"Crazy busy. A reporter from the local paper interviewed me."

Her dad smiled. "You're becoming quite the celebrity."

Zara rolled her eyes. "She said it should be in tomorrow's paper. How about you? How was your day?"

"Not as exciting as yours, I'm afraid."

As they ate, Zara told him about the interview and the little girl who asked the lonely boy to color.

"I have to ask you, honey. Do you like running the daycare? I don't want you to feel obligated. I've had a few inquiries from people interested in purchasing it. So if you've found that it's not quite what you'd expected, don't feel like you can't walk away."

Zara sat up straighter. "No. I mean, yes, I love running the center, and no, don't sell it. I'm enjoying working with the children. At least for now."

After eating, they cleared the table, and Zara put the stones, cards, and bags in separate piles. Her dad put the stones into the bags and handed them to Zara, who attached the card.

"What are you going to do if this really takes off? Look how long it's taking us to put together a hundred stone sets. Imagine a thousand!"

Zara threaded the cord through a hole she'd punched in the card. "That would be a nice problem to have. Someone told me about a local job program for the mentally challenged. They do rote work, mostly putting things together. I thought if I ever needed a lot of help that might be one place to look."

Her dad dropped a stone into a bag. "And you'd be helping the workers, causing more ripples."

"Precisely. They'd earn some money and feel good about doing something useful." Zara tied a card to a bag. "Are you okay with me starting to go through Mom's closet, Dad?"

He sighed. "Take your time. I know it has to be done, but it can be a process. I should have insisted your mother and I go through Johnny's things, but every time I brought it up, we'd argue about it. Eventually, I just stopped mentioning it."

"Everyone handles grief differently, Dad. Mom wasn't ready to let go of Johnny's things. Going into his room, and sitting on his bed, and being surrounded by things that represented his life is comforting. It is for me, anyway. I feel close to him, as if he's there in the room with me. Remove the physical reminders of his life and you have an empty white room—and an empty heart. But the key is to hold on to our memories, both of Johnny and Mom. Both of them died much too young. Life's not fair. In fact, sometimes it downright stinks. But it's the only one we have, so we have to make the most of it."

Zara's dad smiled. "How did my little girl become so smart?"

She patted his arm. "I had a very good teacher."

The next morning as soon as Zara woke up, she ran downstairs to grab the newspaper off the front porch. She hadn't expected her photo to be on the front page, but there it was. A big photo of her smiling, surrounded by a crowd of children. Her heart pounded as she read the article. Weird how it felt like she was reading about someone else. But it was she who'd had this dream and made it happen.

As in the *Times* article, the local reporter interviewed other sources. There was the spokesman for the Runner's Club, saying how excited he'd been when Zara contacted him about giving stones to the wounded veterans participating in the race.

I thought it was a great idea to recognize these guys. They worked so hard to overcome so much. The stone is something they can keep. It's not only a reminder of what they've accomplished but how their accomplishments have impacted others.

The race organizer went on to say how he'd received an e-mail from a Marine who'd recently lost both his legs.

This guy's lying in his hospital bed surrounded by tubes and lines. I'm sure the last thing he was thinking about was racing. But when he saw the race on the six o'clock news, it inspired him. He saw guys with the same injuries, some even worse, doing something he thought he'd never do again—run. That's what these guys do. They inspire others or, as Miss Peede says, cause ripples. They show others, both able-bodied and not, what can be achieved through determination and perseverance.

Zara hadn't expected the tears, but they rolled down her cheeks, washing away any doubt that what she was doing was making a difference.

"Honey, are you all right?" Her dad walked into the kitchen.

Zara sniffed and handed him the paper. His eyes popped when he saw the headline in big, bold type.

THE STONE GIVER.

He sat down to read the article. "I'm so proud of you, sweetie. And your mom and Johnny would be too." He hugged her.

"Thanks, Dad. I can't even begin to describe what I'm feeling. Relief that people get what I'm trying to do. Overwhelmed by all the support. Thankful for the sermon that led to all of this. Scared that I won't be able to keep it going."

Her dad nodded. "You'll be just fine. You know, I've been reading that book you told me about. There's a lot of great advice in it. One line I remember in particular is that you can accomplish anything if you believe it's possible. You've believed this was possible from the beginning. Don't stop believing in yourself now. It's more important than knowledge, training, or schooling, the book authors said. And I agree. So many people fail because they don't believe they can succeed."

Zara smiled. "Thanks, Dad. I needed to hear that."

[174]

He patted Zara on the back. "I didn't tell you anything you didn't already know."

Zara nodded. "But sometimes it's good to be reminded. Even when you believe in yourself, doubt has a way of sneaking in during your weaker moments. I need to remember that those who succeed are those who think they can."

The phone rang, and Zara's dad picked it up.

"I'll tell her, Sandy," he said. "Yes, you can buy the stones on the website listed."

Just as her dad hung up the phone, it rang again. A neighbor called. Then another neighbor. Then a friend.

Zara poured another cup of coffee. "I think you're going to have to stop answering the phone so you can get ready for work."

Her dad buttered his toast. "I think you're right."

Zara finished breakfast and then checked her website. She'd sold ten more stones. Luckily, she and her dad had put together twenty more gift sets than she had orders for the night before. She'd mail them on her way to work.

CHAPTER TWENTY-FIVE

Jack stared at the computer screen. Ever since he'd decided to go to college on the GI Bill, he'd been researching various universities. Under the bill, the government would pay for his tuition and school fees, give him a monthly housing allowance, and give him up to a thousand dollars to use for books and supplies.

He was using an online tool that helped him narrow his career choice. He could search by keywords based on things that interested him or by industry. Or he could enter the name or code of his military classification and the program would suggest similar work.

He opted to search by keywords, entering those that described his dream job. He typed in: *helping others, teaching, exercise, coaching*.

A list of the top twenty civilian careers for helping others, teaching, exercise, coaching popped up. The closest matches were shown first. Exercise physiologist topped the list. He clicked on it to learn more about the career. It would require at least a bachelor's degree.

It appealed to his problem-solving skills. He liked the idea of developing individual exercise programs and analyzing the data to evaluate progress or needed changes. He'd been sort of doing that with Sam, coaching him on how to improve his strength and endurance. It was definitely a career to consider. He thrived on figuring out how to do things better.

He noticed too that along with the list of career options was an Explore More section. He read the note.

You might like a career in one of these industries: health and counseling.

He'd been thinking about mechanical engineering and hadn't given nursing a thought, but maybe he should. He clicked on the health and counseling link, and it took him to a list of other careers. At the top of the list was Acute Care Nurse. Seeing the word "nurse" made him think of Zara. He smiled, wondering what she was doing at that moment.

Second on the list were cardiovascular technologists and technicians. This also appealed to him. Doing electrocardiograms, administering stress tests, and using various devices and instruments to record a patient's cardiac activity seemed like an important profession.

Jack ran his fingers through his hair. The more he explored possible careers the more certain he became that he should pursue a degree in the healthcare field. The problem was which one. Several appealed to him. Maybe he could talk to Zara about it. After all, she had a lot of experience. She'd probably have great advice.

He pulled the Cause a Ripple stone out of his shorts pocket and clutched it. He'd hopefully create some ripples if he did any of these jobs. Funny how important making a difference had become to him. Before Zara, before the stone, he hadn't thought about how his actions affected others. Of course, he never wanted to hurt anyone, but he didn't consider if doing something or saying something would. Now he did.

He always carried the stone in his pocket along with the heart-shaped one Zara had first given him. He found himself touching it throughout the day, a reminder of the impact he had. It could be good or bad — and he wanted it to be good. There had to be a reason why he'd survived the explosion, and he didn't want to screw up the chance he'd been given.

There was a knock at the door.

"Come in."

Sam peeked in. "You're still on the computer?"

"Come in. I need a break."

Jack told Sam about his career search and what he'd found.

"Man, I wish I could do something like that."

"You can," Jack said. "You've got the GI Bill."

Sam waved his hand. "Nah! Don't have the smarts like you."

"Don't sell yourself short," Jack said. "Look what you said about completing a marathon. You never believed you'd ever be able to do it. And you did."

Sam nodded. "But this is different. That's physical stuff. This is brain stuff. I always had trouble in school. Struggled with reading."

Jack listened as Sam described being in elementary school and not understanding what he was reading. "Kids made fun of me. Said I was slow. But I was tested and had normal intelligence. Just had problems processing information. Sort of gave up after that."

"So you're dyslexic?" Jack asked.

"Yeah, that's what they called it."

"My buddy was dyslexic. Heck, it's the most common learning disability. It's nothing to be ashamed of. I'm sure we could find you a tutor. Don't give up on going to school, Sam. You don't have to go to a university. Maybe you'd rather go to a vocational school."

"Do you really think I could do it?"

"Someone special told me a long time ago that if you want to succeed, you will. Winners don't become winners if they never try. Think about it. If you want, I can sit with you and show you a program that matches your interests with possible careers."

"So what did the program tell you?" Sam asked.

Jack smiled. "Healthcare industry. Nurse, exercise physiologist."

"I can totally see that, man. You're great at helping others, taking care of people."

"Thanks. It's given me some things to think about for sure. I'm going to ask Zara about the nursing profession when I see her on Saturday."

"Can you also ask her if she has any hot friends?" Sam laughed.

Jack rolled his eyes and walked to the refrigerator. "Would you like a beer?"

"I thought you'd never ask."

Jack got two beers and handed one to Sam.

"Do you ever wish you were back in the barracks with the guys?" Sam asked.

"Sometimes," Jack said. "I miss the camaraderie. Being in the rehab gym is a lot like it, though. Everyone's always kidding each other, doing stupid, crazy stuff."

"I worry about not fitting in," Sam said. "Take college, for example. Aren't you worried how you'll fit in with a bunch of kids still battling acne?"

Jack laughed. "Actually, the college I was looking at has a resource center for vets. I guess they figure we need a place where we can hang out with guys who understand what we've been through. It's a separate building on campus, and besides free coffee and computers, there's counseling services. Sort of like the peer counselors we have here. Guys who can help you figure out the academic stuff."

"Just keep talking and you'll have me enrolled right along with you." Sam laughed.

Zara opened her mom's walk-in closet. She scanned the beige walls. The clothes were hung according to season, item, and color. Shoes and sweaters were arranged neatly in white wooden cubbyholes. Belts, and scarves, and purses hung from racks mounted to the wall. Nothing was out of place.

Zara walked over to her dad's closet and opened the door. His closet was chaos. Nothing belonged anywhere. Seasons, and items, and colors ran together. Like an artist's palette, Zara was sure his closet had started out neat and orderly, each color occupying its own space. But over time, the colors had inched toward one another. Some bled together. Others were blended on purpose. And yet there was beauty in the chaos, in the palette covered with smudges.

She admired how two people could be so different and yet love one another so much. She thought about Jack. She wondered what his closet looked like. Was he neat or messy? Zara was neat, like her mother. She loved cubbyholes, and bins, and baskets. She found comfort in an organized closet, felt a sense of control. Take away the boundaries and expectations and she floundered in a sea of doubt.

She ran her life in much the same way and felt nervous when someone came into her life and didn't fit into the cubby she had prepared. This was Jack. She knew she couldn't force him into a cubby. That would be like trying to force her gym bag into a cubby meant for a clutch. It would never fit, no matter how hard she pushed, or squeezed, or bent it. She needed to give it space to breathe and stretch.

Zara started removing the clothes, putting them into different bags. One bag would go to an organization that helped women reentering the workforce. Her neighbor volunteered there and was always looking for clothes to give women who were returning to work but didn't have the money to buy a new wardrobe. Another bag would go to an organization that provided free clothes to those in need.

Zara removed a black blazer that still had the price tag dangling from its sleeve. She smiled, wondering how many price tags she'd find. Her mom was a bargain shopper. It was typical of her to buy something at the end of a season and save it for the next year.

She pulled out a brown sweater and held it up to her nose. It smelled like her mom, a citrusy blend with an underlying scent of musk. She hugged the sweater, picturing her mother wearing it. She wasn't going to put this into any bag. She was going to keep this one for herself.

Her dad walked into the bedroom and saw the brown sweater balled up in Zara's arms. "Are you okay?"

Zara nodded.

"Need any help?"

"No, I'm good."

Her dad looked at the bags. "Well, it looks like you're making progress."

"Is there anything you want to keep, Dad? Like a scarf or something?"

He shook his head. "Give it all to charity. Your mother would want that. And let me know when you're done. I'll carry the bags to the car. I'll be in my office working."

Zara's dad left, and she set the sweater aside and went back to sorting clothes. She hadn't expected to finish the closet in one night, but she was moving along at a fast clip. The purses were next. Her mom loved purses. She also loved shoes. And she found great joy in matching her purses and shoes with her outfits.

Growing up, this was one thing Zara's friends had always commented on. "Your mom's purses always match her shoes." Most of her friends' moms had one bag about the size of a small suitcase that bulged with everything a mom might need—bandages, tissues, mints and gum, safety pins, nail clippers, lipstick, powder compact, and perfume.

Zara put most of her mom's purses into the bag containing the dressier clothes. She thought the women returning to the workforce might like a new purse.

She reached for the blue bag in the corner of the closet. She peeked inside. There was a small gift wrapped in white paper topped with a pink bow, along with a card addressed to her. Zara gasped. Her birthday was a month away, but apparently, her mom had already bought her gift. She wondered if she should open it or wait. She decided to open it.

She picked up the card. Her mom never sealed envelopes unless they were being mailed. Instead, she'd tuck the triangular flap inside the card. Zara lifted the flap and pulled out the card. Her chin trembled, and her eyes filled with tears. The card had water ripples, concentric circles emanating from a stone in the shape of a heart. The card's message: *You've made a difference in my life.*

Zara opened the card and read the note her mom had written.

Zara, As soon as I saw this card I thought of you. Keep causing those ripples. You are touching so many lives and making a real difference in the world. I'm proud of you and the young woman you've become. Always remember that those who succeed are those who believe they can. Never doubt yourself or give up on your dreams. They are far too precious, like you.

I love you bunches and bunches.

Mom

Tears flooded Zara's face. She knew her mom hadn't agreed with her decision to leave nursing, and she hadn't realized how much she wanted her mom's blessing. This card was just what she needed. Of course, she knew her mom would support her no matter what, but finding the card and reading what her mom wrote was the affirmation Zara had been desperate for.

She picked up the wrapped box and untied the pink ribbon. She carefully peeled back the wrapping at the seam. She inhaled deeply and took off the lid. Again, her chin trembled. It was a sterling silver pendant enhanced with blue resin enamel. There was a card tucked inside from the artist, explaining the piece was inspired by a pebble being dropped to make ripples in a lake. Zara's chin wobbled as she removed the necklace from the box and put it on. She sniffed.

"Thank you, Mom," she whispered. "I love it."

CHAPTER TWENTY-SIX

Jack opened his desk drawer and pulled out the black journal Zara had given him. He hadn't written in it for a while, and he felt guilty about it. He read his first entry.

I hate the Taliban. They killed my best friend and blew off my legs. If I could, I'd go back and kill every one of them.

Jack's chest tightened. He hadn't realized how angry and full of hate he'd been. He still hated the Taliban. He still wanted to kill every one of them. But he'd worked through his anger over losing his legs and was focusing on what he still had, not what he'd lost.

The more he researched colleges the more confident he became that going back to school was the right choice. Sure, he was scared, but he also knew he couldn't let fear hold him back.

He couldn't wait to see Zara and talk to her about it. Their texts were becoming more frequent, and he looked forward to their nightly phone calls. But he longed to see her in person, wrap her in his arms once again. A night hadn't passed since their time together that he hadn't longed to hold her. He ached for her loving touch and beautiful smile. He thought he was in love before, but he'd never felt about anyone the way he felt about Zara.

From their conversations, it sounded like she was going to stay in Virginia and operate the daycare her mom had started, at least for now. Maybe he'd check colleges in Virginia. That might be a nice state to settle down in—at least for a while.

He picked up his pen and started to write reasons why he liked Zara.

Kind.

Loving.

Sense of humor.

Compassion.

Dedicated.

Loyal.

He looked over what he'd written and realized he hadn't listed any physical attributes. There would have been a time when a hot body and beautiful face would have topped his list. Somewhere along the way, what he looked for in a woman had changed. Zara was the most beautiful woman he'd ever dated, and he felt guilty for not listing it. So he wrote beautiful.

By the time he finished writing in his journal, it was time to go to the track to train with the guys.

Jack's coach walked toward him. "Hi, Jack."

Jack waved.

"Do you want to participate in the Walt Disney World Half Marathon?"

Jack's eyes widened. "Do you think I'm ready for a half?"

"Absolutely," his coach said. "See that guy over there?" He pointed in the direction of the water cooler. "That's Ed. He lost his legs to an IED explosion too. He was the first-place handcyclist in last year's Disney race. He came to talk to you guys about it."

"Thanks. I'll definitely think about it." He walked over to Ed, a lanky guy with a goatee peppered with gray, who was talking with several of Jack's teammates.

Ed held out his hand. "You must be Jack. I hope you'll join us in Disney."

Jack shook his hand. "Sounds like a lot of fun."

"It definitely is. And it's a great course. We start just outside Epcot, run to the Magic Kingdom, and back to Epcot."

"Wow! That's sounds intense."

"Definitely not as intense as the full marathon. That one goes through Epcot, Magic Kingdom, Animal Kingdom, Hollywood Studios, and then through Epcot a second time."

Jack jerked back.

"Don't worry," Ed said, "we'll work up to that."

Zara scanned the bags surrounding her. She'd finished the closet. Her mom's dresser was next and then Johnny's room. But it was too late to start anything else. She went downstairs to get a drink and found her dad in his office.

He looked up. "What's wrong? You look like you've been crying." He pushed out his chair, stood, and walked over to her.

She showed him the card and necklace. "I guess Mom did some early birthday shopping."

Her dad's eyes glistened. "She always knew just the right thing to buy, didn't she?"

Zara smiled. "And she always picked the perfect card. I miss her so much. Johnny too." Her chin trembled, and she couldn't stop the tears from flooding her face."

He hugged her. "I do too, honey. I do too."

Later that night when she crawled into bed, she slept with the necklace under her pillow. In the morning after she showered, she put it on. By the time she walked into the kitchen, her dad had already left for work. He had a breakfast meeting, but made Zara a pot of coffee.

She poured a cup of coffee and scanned the front page of the newspaper lying on the kitchen table. A big photo of flames destroying a home caught her eye. She picked it up to take a closer look. The headline read: *FIVE HOMELESS AFTER FIRE DESTROYS HOME.*

She retrieved a pen and piece of paper and wrote down the address to make donations. Maybe they'd want Johnny's bed and dresser. He'd like knowing a needy family was getting his stuff, she thought.

She picked up her phone and read her messages. There was one from Stacey.

Miss you!

One from Laura.

Can I have your autograph? Two newspaper stories! You're a celebrity.

And one from Jack.

Hope all is well. Looking forward to Saturday. Been searching careers. Nurse?

Zara read Jack's text again. Was he really considering going back to school for nursing?

Zara texted Jack back.

Nurse? We have lots to talk about. See you in two days.

Zara called Laura on her way to work and told her about finding the necklace and card.

"That's super cool!" Laura said. "Your mom always finds the neatest gifts."

"Yeah, I know. So how's work going?"

"Good."

"And Jude?"

"Very good." Laura stressed "very" and held it as long as a whole note. "But what is it about guys and fantasy sports? Take that away and we might find a cure for cancer!"

Zara laughed. "Good luck trying to remove fantasy sports from their lives."

"You're probably right. They couldn't live without fantasy sports any more than they could live without women!"

They talked some more before they hung up, and Zara called Stacy.

"Hey, Stace, got your message. I miss you too."

"Then move back," Stacey said.

Zara laughed. "How's work going?"

"I decided to apply for features editor."

"Really, but won't you miss writing?"

"I will, but I'm ready for a new challenge. And I sort of like the idea of coaching reporters. I've had some great editors and some bad editors in my career, and I think I'd be a good editor, or at least I'd work my butt off trying."

"You'd definitely have a chance to make a difference."

"You mean cause some ripples, don't you?" Stacey asked.

Zara smiled.

"Oh, by the way," Stacey said. "I gave a stone to our receptionist, who just returned to work after battling breast cancer. She loved it. She put it on her desk. Said she wanted to order some for other patients at the cancer center."

"Neat," Zara said. "And I can definitely work with her for a bulk-rate discount."

Zara ended the call and pulled into the center's parking lot. A huge banner hung from the front of the building. It read, CONGRATULATIONS, ZARA!

She bit her lip, trying to dam her tears. When she walked inside, she was greeted by a room full of children and teachers— and her dad. They cheered and presented her with cards and a cake decorated with blue water ripples and the words YOU'RE MAKING A DIFFERENCE!

CHAPTER TWENTY-SEVEN

Sam walked into Jack's apartment. "Are you on the phone with her again?" He rolled his eyes.

Jack hung up his phone. "It's not like we talk all the time."

"You talk every day. And you text in-between talking. And when you're not texting or talking, you're thinking about her. Not that I blame you. She's gorgeous. Too gorgeous for a guy as ugly as you."

Jack picked up a throw pillow and whipped it at Sam. "My stumps aren't as ugly as yours. You did, after all, win the Ugly Stump Contest."

Sam laughed and picked up the pillow and put it back on the couch. "Seriously, though. I'm glad you're happy. That's more than a lot of us can say." He plopped on the couch across from Jack, who was sitting in a chair.

Jack furrowed his brows. "You're not happy, Sam?"

"Not as happy as you. I know things could be worse. It's better to be here, even if I'm lonely, than not. But sometimes I feel like I'll never find someone who'll love me."

"We all have those moments, Sam. But don't give up. Look at me. I never thought I'd see Zara again. And then there she was."

"Yeah, yeah. I know. Don't give up. Heard it all before."

"And you're going to keep on hearing it," Jack teased.

Sam mashed his lips together. "I've been thinking that maybe school wouldn't be such a bad idea. Do you have time to show me that program you were using the other day?"

Jack grabbed his laptop, and Sam sat beside him. "Any idea of what you'd like to do?"

Sam rubbed the stubble on his chin. "Teaching kids might be nice. Kids like me who struggled in school. I've always had a thing for the underdogs."

Jack searched for careers by industry and selected education. "Are you interested in being an elementary school teacher, a middle school teacher, or secondary school teacher?"

"Definitely elementary," Sam said. "Maybe fourth- or fifth-graders. I'd consider middle school but never high school. High school kids think they know everything. At least, I did. Kind of makes me want to go back and apologize for being such an obnoxious jerk."

Jack laughed. "We were all obnoxious jerks."

Sam pointed to the computer screen. "It says the job outlook is bright for elementary teachers, so that's good."

"And listen to this," Jack said. "On the job, you would adapt teaching methods and instructional materials to meet students' varying needs and interests."

"I like that," Sam said. "Figure out what works for a kid so they don't give up like I did."

"I'll send you this link so you can explore more when you have time. There's a lot to read, and you might find something you like more."

"Thanks, man." He patted Jack's shoulder. "You're the brother I never had."

Sam had never talked about his family, and Jack was afraid to bring them up, but his comment opened the door."

"Thanks, Sam," Jack said. "Speaking of family, you never talk about yours."

"That's because I don't have one. Spent most of my life being shuffled from one foster home to the next. Never really had a family until I joined the military. What about you?"

"Had a mom. Wasn't much of a family, though. She worked all the time. She died my senior year in high school. Now, Nate. He had a family. A big old Italian brood that was always hugging and kissing each other. They sort of adopted me."

"That's your buddy that died, right?"

Jack nodded. "He had two sets of grandparents, two sets of great-grandparents, aunts and uncles, and cousins. And six sisters. He was the only boy. I loved hanging out at his house. His sisters were all older and spoiled him, and if I was with him, me too."

"Sounds like fun."

"It was fun. I miss him. I'm going to see his wife and meet his baby for the first time in a few weeks. Been wanting to do it for a while, just had to get up the nerve."

"Are you going to be okay going by yourself?"

"I'm not. Zara's coming along."

Zara sat on Johnny's bed and inhaled deeply, allowing the air to fill her lungs before releasing it slowly through her mouth. Deep breathing calmed her and reduced her stress. She looked around the room. Her dad said she should wait until he could help, but Zara was impatient. Instead of doing it another night when he was free, she decided to get started.

Tackling Johnny's closet wasn't as tough as her mom's. Everything would go to the second-hand shop except for his favorite sweatshirt. Zara pulled the blue fleece over her head and looked into the mirror. Her blonde curls fell over her shoulders. She liked the way she looked in the sweatshirt. She especially liked the way it made her feel—like she was wrapped in a big Johnny bear hug. She took off the shirt and set it aside.

She filled several large garbage bags with clothes before moving to the dresser. She emptied each drawer and smiled when she came across an old prom photo in his sock drawer. He was in a black tux, with a white shirt and red tie. His date, Melissa, wore a red dress. They made a stunning couple. They'd dated Johnny's senior year, but the relationship fell apart when Johnny left for basic training and Melissa left for college. She'd seen Melissa at Johnny's funeral and learned she had a little boy. Zara put the photo in a box she intended to keep.

She wondered if she'd ever have children. She hoped so. And if for some reason she couldn't, she'd adopt.

Zara hoped to finish most of Johnny's room before crawling into bed. She was leaving for Laura's house after she finished work the next day. She left a pile of things she wasn't sure what to do with on the floor beside Johnny's bed. She'd tell her dad to go through them. He might want Johnny's baseball glove, or the first wooden bat he bought him, or Johnny's Boy Scout uniform.

Zara's phone beeped. It was a text from Jack.

Are you free?

Zara typed, *Yes.*

A few seconds later her phone rang. "Hi, Jack."

"Hi. I was wondering if you'd like to go to a baseball game on Saturday. We could go to a game and then out to dinner."

Zara clutched the baseball Johnny caught during an Orioles game. "Sure. I'd love to."

"The team just opened a seven-game home stand, and I haven't seen them play in years."

Zara heard a knock on Jack's end. "I think Sam's here to play poker."

"Do you usually win?" Zara asked.

"It depends. Sometimes yes and sometimes no. Lately, it's been no."

Zara laughed.

"See you soon, Zara. And be careful driving."

Zara coughed. "Now you sound like my dad."

"No! No!" Jack shouted. "I don't want to sound like your dad. I want to sound like your boyfriend. I mean…"

"What did you say?"

"Uh, nothing. Just drive safely."

"That's not what you said," Zara teased. "You said the B word."

"Well, you know, wishful thinking."

Zara smiled. "Good luck playing poker, Jack. I'll see you soon."

Zara hung up the phone and carried the bags downstairs. Her dad said he'd drop them off tomorrow, and if the family needed Johnny's bed and dresser, he'd deliver that as well.

CHAPTER TWENTY-EIGHT

Jack knew Zara was with Laura, and it killed him she was in the same town but not with him. He couldn't wait until tomorrow. He had a bad case of the butterflies.

Jack walked over to Sam's place. He knocked on the door.

"Come in!"

Jack opened the door and saw Sam hovered over his laptop. "Are you on that thing again?"

Sam turned around. "Why do I feel like I have no life when I'm on Facebook? My friends post photos of their vacations, and kids, and projects. Most of them share photos of their food. Makes my life seem so lame."

"Your life's definitely not lame. Remember, you're comparing your life to just what is shown you, and most people only show the good stuff. Besides, don't get like Eugene."

Eugene lived down the hall. Like Sam, Eugene lost a leg in Afghanistan from an IED. Unlike Sam, he played video games all day long.

"I'll never get like Eugene," Sam said. "That guy lives vicariously through others."

"Vicariously? I didn't know you knew such big words."

Sam smirked. "I've been trying to increase my vocabulary. Speaking of Eugene, did you know he created an avatar in an online fantasy world? The guy spends hours on it."

Jack shook his head. "If you ask me, talking with people he's never met in person is not living. It's hiding."

"Tell me about it. I just don't understand when you have real people to talk to, why you'd rather type to someone in another time zone."

"Because it's easy," Jack said. "Start to feel uncomfortable and you can just log off. Real life's not quite like that."

"Let's invite him out," Sam said. "Maybe if we get him drunk, he'll come out of his shell."

Jack laughed. "Might be fun. Then again, might not be. Do you really want to babysit a guy who thought Jack Daniels was a man we met at the bar?"

Sam laughed. "I'd forgotten Eugene thought that."

"Are you going to be around tomorrow?" Jack asked.

"What time?"

"Noon. Zara and I are going to a ballgame and then out for dinner."

"You're inviting me along?"

"No way!" Jack said. "I want her all to myself. But I thought if you were around, maybe we'd stop by if we had time."

"I'd love to see her again," Sam said. "And it'll give me a chance to ask her if she has any hot single girlfriends."

Jack laughed. "How's the career search going?"

"I was on that site before I got on Facebook. I'm still leaning toward teaching elementary school, but I was thinking about special education. Figured with one leg and one arm, I'd be a good role model for the underdog."

Jack patted Sam's shoulder. "You'd be a good role model for anyone."

"It's beautiful," Zara said as she followed Laura around the house she'd purchased. "I love the built-in bookcases. They don't make homes like this anymore."

Laura walked over and pulled down a board. "It's a built-in secretary desk."

"Cool," Zara said. "I've never seen one incorporated into shelves before. My grandma has an antique oak secretary desk with a curved curio cabinet."

"I love those," Laura said. "Does it have a beveled mirror?"

Zara nodded. "And claw feet."

Laura saved the garage for last. She opened the door. "And this is all Jude's."

Zara peeked inside. The garage was packed with stuff, including an old Ford Mustang Jude was rebuilding. "Looks like this must be his heaven."

Laura laughed. "Yeah, he wants to mount a TV on the wall so he can work and still watch football."

Zara rolled her eyes. "Men!"

"Ready to get something to eat? We can catch up over a beer and burger at Joe's."

Zara and Laura went to their old watering hole. Mike, the bartender, walked over to their side of the bar. "Haven't seen you two in a long time."

Laura nudged Zara. "Ah, we've been missed."

"Hi, Mike," Zara said. "I'm just visiting for the weekend."

"It's good to see you both. What can I get you?"

They ordered drafts, and a few minutes later, Mike slid the frosty mugs in front of them.

Laura picked up her glass. "To my bestie. I hope all your dreams come true."

"Likewise," Zara said. She lifted her glass and lightly tapped Laura's. "This beer tastes good. It's been a long time since I had a cold beer."

"I've been drinking too much lately," Laura said. "I need a good cleansing."

"What is it with cleansing?" Zara said. "Everyone's doing it."

"Except me," Laura said. "I've been dirtying."

They both laughed.

Zara loved hanging out with Laura. She always made her laugh, and nothing ever seemed as bad. She was a bit surprised, however, that Laura had finally settled down with one guy. She'd broken plenty of hearts over the years, but Jude seemed to be the one.

Zara shifted in her seat. "How did you know you wanted to be exclusive with Jude?"

Laura sipped her beer. "That's easy. He passed the bar test."

Zara furrowed her brows. "Bar test?"

"Yeah. It works really well. If I go to a bar with a guy and I'm looking around to see who else is there or who might see us together, he fails the bar test. It means I'm still looking and not ready to be exclusive. But if I'm content and want everyone to notice him, then he passes the test."

Zara nodded. "Interesting. I usually resort to a pro slash con list."

Laura held up her hand. "Here's another test. If it's hard for me to introduce him as my boyfriend, that's a sign. Or if the thought of everyone knowing I'm off the market bothers me, I know I'm not ready for an exclusive relationship. With Jude, he passed all the tests. And here's the thing, Zara. It's okay if someone doesn't pass the test. You deserve to be with someone who does, so you keep looking."

"Interesting."

"And," Laura lifted her leg, "I showed him my bunion and my hammer toe."

Zara had just taken a sip of beer and lost it. The beer flew out of her mouth and spritzed the bar top. Mike, who witnessed the great deluge, walked over with a rag and cleaned the counter.

Zara wiped her mouth with a napkin. "Don't do that."

"Do what?" Laura asked.

"Make me laugh while I'm drinking."

"Sorry."

"Well, if you showed him your bunion and hammer toe, you must be in love," Zara said. "I thought you were getting your bunion fixed."

"I plan to, just haven't gotten around to it yet. But I need to. I really do because it's been bothering me."

"Maybe you should stop wearing heels."

"I wear flats sometimes, but then Jude is so much taller that it's impossible to kiss him while standing. Even if I'm on my tippy toes, my mouth is kissing his chest."

Mike walked over. "Do you ladies want menus?"

"I know what I want," Zara said. "I'm been dying to get a Joe's cheesesteak."

"Good choice. I think I'll go with the cheeseburger sub."

Mike walked away, and Zara turned serious. "So you and Jude are really doing well, it seems."

"Yeah. For the most part. We have our moments, but don't we all? Sometimes I think he loves that broken down Mustang more than me. He certainly spends more time with that heap of metal."

Zara laughed. "Maybe you should tell him how you feel."

"I don't want to be too needy," Laura said. "Besides, I know how important restoring the Mustang is. It was a project he and his dad had started. His dad died before they got too far into it, and Jude has always wanted to finish it. So I get that. Enough about me and Jude. Tell me about Jack."

"There's not much to tell. I haven't seen him since New York. Been texting and talking on the phone, though."

"That's promising."

Zara sighed. "Since I've been out of the dating scene for a while, I'd forgotten how much work it is."

Laura sipped her drink. "I always hated dating. I always just wanted to be in a relationship."

"Funny in a way," Zara said, "that in so many aspects of life, we throw ourselves into getting what we want—a college degree, a job, a house. But when it comes to finding someone to spend the rest of our life with, we don't think it should take any work."

"And it's probably the most important decision we'll ever make," Laura said.

Zara sipped her beer. "True. I just have to remind myself I didn't become a nurse without many years of school and I can't be in a relationship without going through the early stages of dating."

Laura raised her glass. "To my bestie. I hope you find your soul mate."

Zara smiled. "I hope I do too."

CHAPTER TWENTY-NINE

Zara texted Jack when she pulled into the parking lot to let him know she had arrived. His apartment was on the second floor, and he met her at the entrance to the building. There were some guys sitting in the lobby, and when Zara walked in dressed in jeans, a tight white shirt, and strappy sandals, they turned to look. Jack greeted her with a hug.

"Sorry it took me a little bit longer than I'd expected," Zara said. "Traffic was horrible in town. Must be a lot going on."

Jack took Zara's arm and led her to the elevator around the corner from the gawking guys. "I told Sam we'd pop in to say hello before we left, if that's okay."

Zara nodded. "Sure. You lead, I'll follow."

They took the elevator to the second floor, turned right, and walked down the hall. Jack knocked on Sam's door.

"Unless you're a gorgeous chick, go away!" Sam yelled.

Jack knocked again.

"Okay, okay. Come in."

Jack and Zara walked in.

Sam was sitting at the kitchen table with his computer and looked up. "I said the gorgeous chick could come in, not you!"

Jack and Zara laughed.

"Remember Zara, Sam?"

Sam stood and walked over. "That's like asking me if I remember the most gorgeous chick I've ever seen. Of course I remember her." Sam held out his hand to shake hers.

Zara smiled. "And I remember you. Of course, I feel as though I know you really well since Jack talks about you so much."

Sam cocked his head. "Good or bad?"

"Good. It's always good."

Sam flashed a thumbs-up. "Do you have any single friends as gorgeous as you looking for a hot date with a one-legged, one-armed man?"

Zara laughed. "No single friends in the area, sorry. But with your winning personality, I don't think you'll have any problems finding someone."

Sam stood straighter. "Why thank you, ma'am."

"Ma'am? Ma'am? Do I look like a Ma'am?"

Sam's face turned as red as the polish on Zara's toes. "You don't look a day over sixteen."

"Nice recovery," Jack teased.

Zara smiled. "Ma'am is fine. But I'd prefer if you called me Zara."

"It's a deal."

Jack pointed to the computer. "Are you on Facebook again?"

"As a matter of fact, I am. I just took a quiz that told me how many women I've had relationships with based on my taste in movies."

Jack laughed. "How many?"

"I'd rather not say."

"See, I told you Sam is crazy," Jack told Zara.

"He's fun," Zara said. "Reminds me a lot of Laura."

"Is she taken?" Sam asked.

"Yes," Zara said.

"Well, if it doesn't work out, tell her you know a great guy who, despite having one arm and one leg, can love like crazy."

Zara chuckled. "Will do."

Jack put his arm around Zara. "We'd better be going. We'll probably miss the first inning as it is."

By the time Zara and Jack pulled into the stadium parking lot, it was the top of the second inning.

"Do you want to grab a drink on the way to our seats?" Jack asked.

"Sounds good."

Zara followed Jack through the concourse toward the entrance to their seats. They found a stand selling beer and jumped in line. A blast rang out, and Jack fell to his knees. The boom triggered memories of the explosion that blew off his legs.

He clutched his chest. His heart pounded. He gasped for air. Sweat pooled on his forehead.

Zara knelt and patted his back. "It's okay, Jack. It's just a panic attack. You're okay. You're with me."

Jack shook and sucked in air.

Zara sat on the concrete floor and took him in her arms, just like she used to do. "Look at me, Jack. Focus. Let's breathe together."

Jack looked into Zara's eyes.

"Good. Now breathe with me."

People around them whispered.

"What's wrong with him?"

"Should we call 911?"

"It started when the mascot fired the cannon after the homerun."

"Poor guy."

"That dude's weird."

Zara looked up at the crowd that was beginning to form. "He was in Afghanistan. He lost both his legs in a roadside explosion.

The cannon triggered a flashback. Please leave us alone. I'm a nurse. I'll take care of him."

The security guard walked over. "You heard what the lady said. He's a soldier. Give him some space."

The guard started to clear everyone away while Zara continued to hold Jack, rocking him gently back and forth. Eventually, his heart rate slowed and he found it easier to breathe.

"Let's get out of here, Jack," Zara said. "We'll come again another day."

Zara helped Jack up and got him to her car with the security guard's help.

"Take care, buddy," the security guard said. "And thank you for serving."

By the time they returned to Jack's apartment, the attack had passed but he was exhausted.

"Sorry I'm a lousy date."

"You're not lousy," Zara said. "Neither of us expected a cannon to fire. It was unsettling for me too. Why don't you rest for a while, and we'll go out for dinner later?"

"Only if you rest with me," Jack said.

Zara helped Jack to bed and crawled in beside him.

"Just when I think it's getting better, something happens, reminding me that this hell will never end."

Zara brushed back Jack's hair. "I understand how debilitating memories triggered by sights, sounds, and smells can be. It's common, Jack. It happens to me sometimes too."

"Really?"

"It happened just last week. I was trying on clothes in a fitting room at my favorite store, and I needed to get a bigger size. As I walked out of the dressing room, I saw a mother hand her daughter clothes. 'Try these on,' she'd said. The scene triggered memories of Mom and me shopping together. She'd always get me another size if I needed it, just like this mother was doing. I ducked into a stall and bawled my eyes out."

"I think that's the worst part." Jack ran his fingers through his hair. "It comes on so fast, and I spin out of control."

"Yes," Zara said. "And there often isn't a way to avoid the external triggers. But that's why we have to learn ways to cope, to lessen the impact. For me, deep breathing helps. Most people don't breathe correctly. They use their chest and shoulders, which causes short, shallow breaths."

"You sound like a nurse," Jack teased.

"I guess I'll always be a nurse at heart."

"Can you show me how?" Jack asked.

Zara sat up in the bed. "Place your hand on your stomach. When you breathe in, your stomach should expand. When you breathe out, your stomach should fall. Try it."

Jack did as Zara had instructed, placing his hand on his stomach, breathing in and then out.

"See the difference?" Zara asked. "When you're having an attack, breathe in deeply, making sure your stomach rises and falls. Short, shallow breaths can increase your stress and anxiety. I can show you some other coping strategies if you want."

"I'd like that," Jack said. "But I just want to rest my eyes for a few minutes."

"Close your eyes. I'll be here when you wake up."

Zara lay beside Jack and watched him sleep. Eventually, she fell asleep too, and when she woke up two hours later, Jack was watching her.

Zara stretched. "How long have you been watching me?"

"Five, maybe ten minutes. You're beautiful even when you sleep."

Zara felt her face become warmer. "Thanks."

Jack leaned in to kiss Zara, and she didn't pull away.

CHAPTER THIRTY

Zara looked at the clock on the wall. "It's almost seven—no wonder I'm starving."

"Me too."

"Should we order in or go out?"

"Since we have reservations, let's go out," Jack said. "Besides, I don't want everything I've planned to be a bust." He kissed the top of Zara's head. "I don't think I've ever apologized to you."

Zara propped herself up on her elbow. "For what?"

"For throwing the stone."

Zara smiled. "My timing was off. I should've waited, but I wanted you to have it before I left."

"I'm glad you didn't wait. That stone got me through so much. When the days were dark, I'd clutch the stone and think of you. You were the light."

Zara leaned down to kiss Jack before scampering to the bathroom to freshen up. When she returned, Jack was sitting on the edge of the bed preparing to put on his prosthetic legs.

"Let me help you." Zara knelt in front of him.

"I'd never thought I'd feel comfortable around a woman ever again. But with you, it's so different. You aren't turned off by my limbs."

Zara smiled. "Jack, your limbs are part of who you are. I don't care for you because of your chiseled abs, tight torso, and thick biceps. Or because you have limbs instead of legs. I care for you because of what's in your heart." She reached up and touched his chest.

Jack's eyes turned glassy. "I don't know what to say. You're more than I ever dreamed of, and I don't want to lose you. I want to keep seeing you and see where this takes us."

"Who said I'm going anywhere?"

"Does that mean you'll stay?"

"It means I want to see where this goes too. Of course I can't stay. I have a daycare center to run, but I'm not that far away."

"I could move to where you are. I've been looking at colleges there."

Zara rolled up his prosthetic sock on his left limb. "You have?"

Jack nodded. "Just doing research. There are some good nursing programs near you."

She rolled the liner over his stump sock. "There are some very good ones." She picked up the other prosthetic sock and rolled it over his limb.

Jack smiled. "You're good at this."

Zara shrugged. "I've had a lot of practice."

Zara finished rolling up his liner and handed Jack one of his legs. He put on his legs and stood. "The bionic man is ready."

Zara sipped her wine. "You were right. The food here is amazing.

"I thought you'd like the chicken marsala. It's one of my favorites. Want to try a bite of my chicken afurmicato?"

"It does look delicious. What's in it?"

"Spinach, sundried tomatoes, roasted red peppers, and smoked cheese."

"Mmm, smoked cheese. I'll try a little bite."

Jack jabbed a piece of pasta and handed his fork to Zara.

She slid the fork into her mouth, pulled it out, and handed it back to him. "You're right. It is delicious." She looked down at her plate. "I'm getting full, and I've only eaten half of my dish."

"Leave room for dessert," Jack said. "The crème brûlée is excellent."

Zara rubbed her stomach. "I'm so glad you brought me here. I've driven down this road so many times, and I've never noticed this tiny restaurant. I guess that's because it sits back from the road."

Jack winked. "Sometimes the best things are right in front of our eyes."

Zara struck a pose. "Like me?"

"Oh, no. From the moment you walked into my hospital room, I noticed you. I was in so much pain, so broken, but I noticed you. When you left, I thought I'd never see you again."

Zara smiled. "Funny sometimes how life works out. You think you're headed in one direction only to find a sharp curve in the road."

Jack reached for Zara's hand. "Do you like the curve?"

Zara bit her lip. "I very much like the curve. How about you?"

"I very much like every single one of your curves."

Zara smiled. "Somehow I don't think we're talking about the same curves."

Jack was going to say more but stopped flirting when the waitress stopped by their table. "Can I get you anything for dessert?"

Zara rubbed her stomach. "I'm stuffed."

The waitress pointed to her plate. "Would you like me to box that up?"

"Yes, please. And I'll take a cup of coffee."

The waitress turned to Jack. "And what about you, sir?"

"How about the crème brûlée, and I'll have some coffee also."

The waitress picked up Zara's plate and headed toward the kitchen.

When the crème brûlée came, Jack insisted Zara try it. He dipped his spoon into the crème brûlée and handed it to her.

She licked her lips. "You're right. It's delicious."

They were enjoying their coffee when Zara's old boyfriend walked in. He immediately saw her and headed to her table.

"Hi, Zara."

She smiled. "Hi, Chris."

"And you're Jack, right?"

Jack nodded.

"Congratulations on the marathon." He shook Jack's hand.

"Thanks."

Chris turned to Zara. "And everyone's been talking about Cause a Ripple. You must be really happy."

"I am. It's a dream come true. How's Tania?"

"Great. I'm here to pick up dinner. Guess I should do that before it gets cold. Take care, Zara. And you too, Jack."

Chris walked to the counter to get his take-out.

"So that's him?" Jack asked.

"Who?"

"Your old boyfriend. Pete pointed him out in the gym one day. First I ever talked to him, though."

Zara sipped her coffee. "That was ages ago."

"Do you still think about him?"

"No. That was over a long time ago, and it wasn't the type of relationship that was going to go anywhere."

"What about ours?"

Zara smirked. "Are you jealous, Jack Quinlan?"

Jack shrugged. "Maybe a little."

"You look cute when you're jealous."

Jack took Zara's hands and leaned toward her. He stared into her green eyes. "I'm falling for you, Zara, and I need to know if you think I have any shot at maybe becoming more."

Zara blinked. "I fell for you a long time ago, Jack. I'd say you have a very good chance."

When they got back to Jack's apartment, Zara brought up Jack's interest in a nursing career.

"I want to help guys like you helped me. I want to take care of them the way you took care of me."

"It won't be easy," Zara said.

"I know, and I might fail, but I have to try."

"Then I'll help you study and prepare. You have a long road ahead of you."

"I know, but it seems to me I have a huge advantage." He tickled Zara. "I have you."

Zara texted Laura after realizing it was almost midnight and it became obvious that she and Jack still had a lot to talk about. Laura texted back three emoticon hearts, and Zara returned a text with a smiley face. Then she snuggled next to Jack and laid her head on his chest, listening to his beating heart and feeling like it was hers.

CHAPTER THIRTY-ONE

Zara called Stacey when she got home and filled her in.

"Oh! My! It finally freakin' happened. You've had the hots for him since the day you met him."

"I've never felt this way about any guy ever before. We connect so completely. I'm happier than I ever thought I could be. But I'm scared too."

Stacey responded in a sharp tone. "Don't you dare back away from this one, girlfriend."

"I don't plan to, but it scares me to want someone as much as I want him. It's like I lose all control and the only thing that matters is Jack and making him happy."

"You definitely sound like you're in love," Stacey said. "And you're also making me feel like crap, because I definitely don't feel that way about Tony."

"I thought you really liked him."

"I do," Stacey said. "But when I listen to you, I can hear your love for Jack. The way you talk about him, the way you describe what it's like being with him. I don't feel that way about Tony. I enjoy being with him, but if we were to break up tomorrow, it wouldn't be the end of my world. And I think that's telling. Listening to you has made me think about some things."

"I'm sorry," Zara said. "I certainly didn't intend to make you second guess your relationship with Tony."

"I'm glad we're talking," Stacey said. "You'd made me realize that I should never settle. Tony's a great guy. I'm just not sure he's the right one for me."

Zara heard the back door open. "Sounds like Dad's home. I'll talk to you later. And, Stace, don't make any abrupt decisions. Tony's a great guy. Maybe you just need to give it some time."

Zara hung up the phone.

"Hi, sweetie," her dad said.

"Hey, Dad."

"Who were you on the phone with? Laura? Or Stacey?"

"Stacey, but both told me to tell you hi."

"So how was your visit?"

"Awesome."

Her dad stared at her. "It's so good to see you smile. I mean really smile. The way you used to."

"Thanks, Dad. I haven't been this happy in a long time. I spent some time with Jack when I visited Laura."

"How about we get a glass of wine and go into the living room to talk. I want to hear all about it."

Zara followed her dad into the living room, and they sat down.

"So, you really like him, don't you?" Zara's dad asked.

Zara nodded.

"Are you sure you're not mistaking pity for romantic feelings?"

"I'm sure, Dad. From the very beginning, I felt a connection. After I left Walter Reed, a day hadn't passed when I didn't think about Jack, but I knew I was his nurse and so I could never be more. Then I went to the banquet. Believe me, Jack was the last person I'd expected to see. But there he was, standing tall on his prosthetic legs and incredible looking in his suit."

Zara's dad listened as she told him the rest of the story, minus the intimate conversations."

"So he's moving here?" her dad asked.

Zara nodded.

"Are you moving in together?"

Zara shook her head. "Separate apartments. We want to take things slowly. And I need my own space. Besides, you know how I feel about living together before marriage."

"I'm happy for you, honey. But you know I need to meet this man who's captured by daughter's heart."

Zara set down her wine glass and jumped up to hug her dad. "You will, Dad. Promise."

"And I'll still help you with Cause a Ripple. Speaking of which, I put together a hundred gift sets over the weekend. Thought I'd try to get ahead."

"Omigosh! I haven't checked the website since I left." Zara pulled out her cell phone and checked the site. "There's an order for a hundred!"

Her dad smiled. "Looks like you're causing quite a few ripples."

"Thanks, Dad. Maybe there's truth in marrying your passion with your job. If you love what you do, it doesn't seem like work at all."

That night, Zara went to bed and couldn't stop thinking about Jack. Their time together had been incredible. He was so tender, so giving. She replayed their time together over and over in her mind. Their passionate kisses. The way he touched her and made her feel beautiful and wanted. It was perfect.

She couldn't sleep, so she pulled out the pill puzzle she'd put in her nightstand drawer. She held it with both hands, gently tilting it, attempting to get the tiny silver balls into the tiny holes. She bit her lip as she got one in, then another, and another. She gasped. She'd managed to get all of the balls in the holes—at the same time.

CHAPTER THIRTY-TWO

Zara turned off the car and looked over at Jack. "You got this. I'm going to be right by your side."

Jack wrung his hands. "I haven't seen Alicia in a long time. We were home on leave, and she had a birthday party for him. I feel bad I didn't reach out sooner."

Zara took Jack's hands. "Look, Jack. Stop beating yourself up. You're here now. We'll do this together. You know Alicia wants to see you. She told you that when you called."

Zara glanced toward the white, two-story house and saw a head peek out of the front window. "She's looking out, Jack."

Jack inhaled deeply and blew the air out of his mouth. He opened his sweaty fist, revealing the gold four-leaf clover Nate had given him. "I'm ready."

Zara climbed out of the car, walked around to the passenger side, and opened the door for Jack. Jack crawled out, took her hand, and squeezed it. "Thanks for coming with me."

"I wouldn't have it any other way."

When they reached the porch, Alicia opened the door holding a baby bundled in blue with a colorful teething ring in his hand. Alicia started crying, and Jack started crying, and pretty soon everyone was crying. They walked into the living room, and Jack introduced Zara.

"It's so nice to finally meet you," Zara said. "I've heard so much about you and Nate."

Alicia sniffed. "Thanks. It's nice to meet you too. And, Jack, it's so, so good to see you."

Because Alicia was holding the baby, they could only half hug.

"You look great," Jack said. He thought she looked like the blonde fourteen-year-old Nate fell in love with his junior year in high school. Long legs, a body with curves in all the right places, and a smile that lit up any room she walked into.

"Thanks," Alicia said. "You do too. Please, have a seat."

Zara sat on the chair facing the sofa where Alicia and Jack sat.

Alicia pointed to Jack's legs. "Was it tough learning to walk on those?"

Jack nodded. "Probably the hardest thing I ever had to do." Jack couldn't stop looking at the baby. "I see he has Nate's hair."

Alicia laughed. "Yeah, he had so much black hair when he was born everyone commented on it. Would you like to hold him?"

"He's so small. I don't want to hurt him."

"You won't. Make a cradle with your arms." Alicia placed the baby in Jack's arms. "See, that's not so bad."

Jack held out his finger, and baby Nate wrapped his tiny fingers around it. "Hey, Nathan. It's good to finally meet you. Your daddy was my best friend."

Alicia reached for the box of tissues. "We're going to have to make sure we tell him all about Nate. What a great guy he was." Alicia started sobbing, and Zara walked over to her and rubbed her shoulder. "I'm sorry," Alicia said. "I promised myself I wouldn't cry."

"It's okay," Zara said. "You're right. You and Jack will have lots of great things to tell Nathan about his dad."

"Like the time we sold boxes of rotten cherries," Jack said.

Alicia smiled. "Now, there's a story I haven't heard in a while."

"Remember the time your parents were out of town and you had a party and…"

Alicia playfully slapped Jack's leg. "We're only going to tell baby Nate nice stories."

"I think if Nate were here, he'd say that was a great story." As soon as Jack said it, he wished he could stuff it back in his mouth. "I'm sorry."

Alicia waved. "No, it's all right. Really. It's hurts to reminisce, but it also feels good. Sometimes, I'm afraid that I'll forget what Nate looked like or how his voice sounded. And I never want to forget. The other day, I took the baby to his grave and spread a blanket out in front of it. It was such a beautiful day, and I just wanted to be near Nate with the baby. So I lay down on the blanket with the baby, and for a little bit, I felt closer to him."

Zara's chin trembled as she listened to Alicia.

Jack wiped his eyes on his shoulder. "Oh, I almost forgot. I have something for you."

Zara stood. "Do you mind if I hold Nathan?"

Alicia shook her head. "Not at all."

Zara took Nathan in her arms and sat back down on the chair. Jack stuffed his hand into his shorts pocket, pulled out the gold four-leaf clover, and held it up. "Nate gave this to me not long before he died. He wanted his baby to have it." Jack bit his lip, trying to keep himself composed.

He'd pictured this scene over and over since waking up in Walter Reed to stumps instead of legs. What would he tell Alicia? How would he ever be able to face her, knowing he was the one who'd driven over the pressure plate? The horror of that day rushed back as the words flew out of his mouth.

"Alicia." He sobbed. "I'm so sorry. I wish Nate was here and I'd been the one who died."

Alicia took Jack's hands. "Look at me, Jack. I don't blame you for what happened to Nate. No one does. Nate loved you. You were his brother. You were inseparable from the time you two met in kindergarten."

Listening to Alicia caused an explosion of emotions in Jack, and he cried like he'd never cried before. Alicia took Jack in her arms, and he sobbed into her shoulder while Zara, holding Nathan, cried too.

"The last thing Nate would want is for you to feel guilty because you survived," Alicia said.

Jack sniffed and reached for some more tissues. "Are you doing okay? I mean, be honest."

"I have good days and bad days. The good days are becoming more frequent, and I'm thankful I have the baby. He's a part of Nate that I will always have. Nate's family is great. I couldn't ask for a better support network, especially since my parents moved away."

"Yeah," Jack said. "I wasn't sure you'd stay here."

"It just didn't seem right to leave Nate's family. Besides, my parents visit often, and we talk every day."

"I'd like to see Nate's family."

"They'd like to see you too, Jack. When I told them you were coming, they wanted to be here too. But I asked them to give us this time alone. His mom said to tell you she loves you and when you're feeling up to it, she wants to cook for the whole family, like she used to do."

"I'd like that," Jack said. "I really miss those times. She always made me feel as if I were her second son."

"Well, I know she's feels the same way. His sisters do too."

They reminisced some more while Zara gave Nathan his bottle. There were moments of tears and moments of laughter. But they were all good moments.

Zara looked down at the baby in her arms. "Nathan's asleep."

Alicia stood. "I'll put him in his crib." She took the baby to the nursery.

"How do you feel?" Zara asked Jack.

Jack sighed. "Exhausted." He got up and walked over to the fireplace mantel, and Zara joined him. A photo of Nate in military attire sat next to a photo of his son. Jack pulled the Cause a Ripple stone from his pocket, kissed it, and placed it between the two photos. He touched Nate's photo. "I miss you, buddy. Your son is beautiful. You'd be proud."

A year later

Jack stood at the front of the church with Sam and Tom. He watched Stacey and Laura float down the aisle, past Pete and so many others he and Zara had gotten to know over the past year. Alicia and Nate's family smiled at him from the first pew. They were his family, and he wanted them to sit where his mom would have.

Alicia was right. No one blamed him for Nate's death—they just wanted to love him.

When the bridesmaids had made it down the aisle and taken their places, the organist started to play *The Wedding March*. Everyone turned to watch as Zara and her dad walked arm in arm. Jack thought Zara looked like an angel in her mother's wedding dress, the lacey train cascading from her tiny waist and trailing behind her.

So many good things had happened in the past year that Jack was terrified he'd wake up to find it was all a dream. He'd finished his first year of college, Cause a Ripple had taken off, and running the foundation had become a full-time job for Zara. She had hired someone else to run the daycare center.

Jack continued to compete in marathons with Sam, who was also in college, studying to be an elementary school teacher.

With Zara's help, Jack beat back the demons that haunted him at night and reared their ugly heads during the day. They still had a long way to go, but they both knew they were stronger and better together.

Jack visited Nathan as much as he could and marveled at how fast he was growing. Lately, he and Zara had been talking about starting a family.

"That's what the honeymoon is for," Zara had said.

Jack thought she was teasing.

She wasn't.

A stone is dropped
And we don't realize
The ripples it creates
Can last a lifetime

Also available from Buffy Andrews and Prism Book Group...

Ella's Rain

Ella is consumed by grief when her Grandma Dorothy dies. Left with Grandma's ashes in an alabaster urn, Ella dreams of rubbing it like a magic lamp and Grandma suddenly appearing.

But it's only a dream.

To protect herself from experiencing this kind of heartache ever again, Ella pulls away from Trey, the love of her life. Better to leave him than to lose him, she thinks.Slowly Ella learns to live again as she reads the letters Grandma left behind — one for every day of the coming year.

Please enjoy this sample...

Ella stared at the alabaster urn the funeral director had given her. It was hard to believe that Grandma had become nothing more than a pile of white ashes. She longed to feel her grandma's thick arms around her and to smell her sweet perfume that hung in the air like an August fog. How does a cream puff of a lady become nothing more than a bag of dust, she wondered.

Cancer. That evil C word. The word she had lived with for almost a year. The evil thing that had devoured Grandma like a vulture devours a dead carcass, gorging itself until its crop bulges and leaves nothing but splintered bones behind.

It was so unfair, Ella thought. Grandma Dorothy was all she had. Now her beloved Dorothy was gone, off to an emerald city from which she would never return. And Ella was left with nothing but the sage alabaster urn Grandma had picked out before she died. Picked out like everything else.

The hymns that would be sung. The biblical passages that would be read. Even the flowers that would sit beside the urn on the pedestal table. She'd picked everything out as if she'd been planning a picnic, and Ella hated her for it.

Sometimes, Ella couldn't stand Grandma's optimism, and she'd escape to her room. She'd tell Grandma she had to study, but she never did. She'd lie on her bed, stare at the ceiling, and think, and remember, and pretend—pretend that Grandma was in the kitchen singing her favorite Doris Day song and making macaroni and cheese.

Ella could hear Grandma's voice in her head. *Whatever will be will be.*

She started to cry. Screw *whatever will be will be*, she thought. What about what I want? Then she started to panic, afraid that Grandma's voice would fade like her mother's, and father's, and sister's. No matter how hard she tried, Ella no longer heard their voices.

They'd died when Ella was six. Killed in an accident on the way home from the zoo. *Crash Kills Family of Three*, the newspaper headline had said.

Ella could still remember that day, as if it was yesterday or the day before instead of eleven years ago. Ella had a stomach virus and was too sick to go. She'd spent the night throwing up and eventually fell asleep in her mother's arms next to the white porcelain tub. Grandma had watched her while the rest of Ella's family met her mom's friend for their annual zoo outing.

Ella was so upset she couldn't go that she cried the whole way through *Willy Wonka and the Chocolate Factory*—her favorite movie.

Even watching Augustus Gloop fall into the chocolate river and being sucked out by the extraction pipe, and gum-chewing Violet Beauregarde blowing up like a balloon, didn't make her laugh.

Grandma promised to take her to the zoo when she felt better, but Ella still cried. She wanted to see the monkeys with Sissy. And the bears, giraffes, and tigers.

After her parents and sister died, Ella wanted nothing to do with the zoo. Grandma brought it up a few times. She thought it would be good for Ella to go, but Ella refused. She wasn't going anywhere near the zoo and, after a time, Grandma stopped asking.

Grandma's best friend, Maddie, put her arms around Ella. Everyone else had left after the funeral service—her best friend, Emily, even Trey. Secretly, Ella had wanted him to stay, but she kept pushing him away. She'd been doing that for months.

It was better that way, she thought. Everyone she loved she'd lost. Losing Trey would be too much. She had to protect herself from ever feeling this way again. And if turning away from Trey was what she needed to do to protect herself, well, then that's what she had to do.

"Ready?" Maddie asked.

No, Ella wasn't ready. She wasn't ready to move into Maddie's house. She adored Maddie. Loved her. She was like the aunt Ella never had, but Maddie wasn't Grandma.

However, Ella had no choice. Grandma had planned everything. Just like the hymns, and the readings, and the flowers. Maddie, a retired school teacher, would become Ella's guardian and see her through her last year of high school and college. That was the plan—Grandma's plan. As much as Ella hated it, she knew it was the only way.

"I hope that even in the rain," Grandma always told her, "you find the sun."

Screw the sun, Ella thought as she grabbed her coat and followed Maddie to the front door. There was no sun in sight. Only a razor-blade rain that sliced her aching heart and chilled her to the bone.

Look for *Ella's Rain* at all major eBook retailers, or learn more at the Prism Book Group website at: http://www.prismbookgroup.com!

ABOUT THE AUTHOR

Buffy Andrews is an author, blogger, journalist, and social-media maven. She writes middle-grade, young adult, contemporary romance and women's fiction.

She lives in south-central Pennsylvania with her husband, Tom; two sons, Zach and Micah; and wheaten cairn terrier, Kakita. She is grateful for their love and support and for reminding her of what's most important in life.

Thank you for your Prism Book Group purchase! Visit our website to enjoy free reads, great deals, and entertaining, wholesome fiction!

http://www.prismbookgroup.com

Made in the USA
Middletown, DE
11 January 2020